Praise for Roger Real Drouin and NO OTHER WAY

"Drouin's debut novel...is lyrical and poetic, soft and whispering, telling us, 'It is a hope as light and fragile as the shadows flying through the tall grass.' "—*Grey Sparrow Journal*

"His prose is fluid and poetic. Drouin is definitely a writer to keep an eye on."—*Martin Lastrapes, author of Inside the Outside, winner of the Paris Book Festival Grand Prize.*

"...writes with a great sensitivity for detail...brings the reader deep into a natural setting."—*Murray Dunlap, author of Bastard Blue and Alabama.*

"Drouin writes about nature with an innate sense of poetry...*No Other Way* soars for a thousand miles."—*Steel Toe Review*

"Roger Real Drouin manages to capture the natural beauty of nature in nothing more than words and to do so in abundance....a gem in the literary world."—*Dan Schwartz, author of No Cure for Nature*

"...beautifully textured images...staggering metaphors...magic still exists."—*Sheldon Lee Compton, author of The Same Terrible Storm*

Roger Real Drouin

No Other Way

Roger Real Drouin is a journalist and teacher. He received his MFA in Creative Writing from Florida Atlantic University. Roger's short stories and essays have appeared in the journals *The Litchfield Review, Grey Sparrow Journal, Crosstimbers, Leaf Garden Press, Pindeldyboz, EarthSpeak Magazine, Steel Toe Review, Mobius, MadSwirl, Platte Valley Review, The Explicator,* and *The Northville Review.*

Roger writes about his outdoor adventures on his blog www.rogersoutdoorblog.com.

Also by Roger Real Drouin

Sparrow Creek, Forthcoming

NO OTHER WAY

Roger Real Drouin

Moonshine Cove Publishing, LLC

ISBN: 978-1-937327-064
Library of Congress Control Number: 2012938606

Book design by Moonshine Cove Publishing; Greg Stahl cover photograph of unnamed peak and Nick Athanas front and back cover photograph of Whimbrel used with permission.

ACKNOWLEDGEMENTS

I couldn't have finished this novel without my fiancé Rachel's help, encouragement and patience.

I would like to thank my mom for always supporting me.

I also wish to thank my loyal hound Sandy for her companionship during the daily writing of this novel.

I am also grateful for the support from my father Roger, my sister Jessica, my stepfather Dennis, as well as Rose and Frank, and all of my family. I am honored to thank those close friends who provided invaluable advice or just let me vent when this writer's journey got rough: Ryan Downey, Ben Crespi, David Dinatali, Heidi Kurpiela Bardi, Ricci Shryock, Beau Ewan, and Simone Puleo. A special thanks to Mary Ann Hogan for advice over coffee and encouragement when I needed it. I would also like to thank my mentors Professor A. Papatya Bucak, Dr. Andrew Furman, and Dr. Taylor Hagood.

My writing was set in motion a long time ago by those New England fishing and hiking trips with my Uncle Emo, who was never too busy to go on an adventure with me. He taught me to respect and love our natural places.

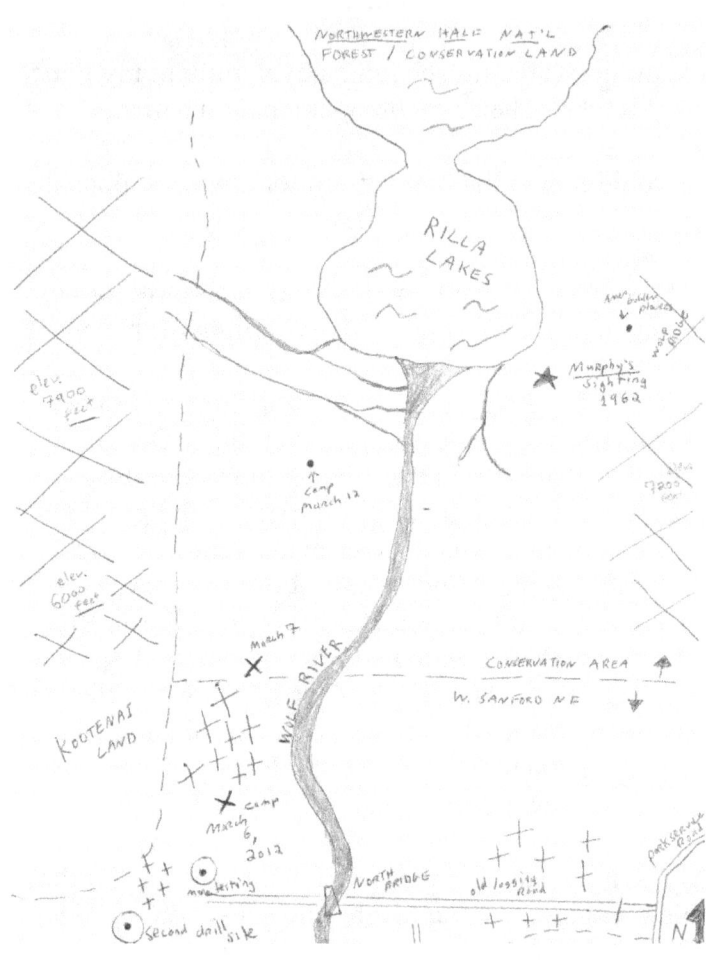

Sketch Map from Samuel's Field Notebook,
Rilla Lakes Area, Wilson Sanford National
Forest

CHAPTER ONE

Early September, four years ago

Under the clouds like gray broken plates. Here he was, chasing true scientific endeavor.

The photographer of birds hiked further into the 36,000-acre South Carolina pine bluff, the wind heavy with that wet coldness. The rain would be coming soon.

He knew he was chasing a ghost.

He hiked further along the two-rutted park service trail. The rain would come within the hour, he thought, but despite the pale white-gray sky, it felt good to be in the field again. The strong coffee in his thermos and the new snug-fitting hiking boots were two modest checks in the positive column. From the boots to the cotton-canvas pants, and the thick flannel and heavy rucksack, the photographer was prepared for the weather, and the motion of the hike kept him warm.

He was searching for the Northern Stilted Curlew, one of the world's rarest birds, a species last documented in 1962. This arctic shorebird was what is called a grail bird—it may or may not exist. In Samuel's thick four-volume *Master Guide to Birding*, the Curlew was listed as "probably extinct." A color sketch showed the sturdy, dull-looking bird capable of flying the longest annual migration of any species, other than a handful of sea birds that can stop and rest on the water. Every September, the Curlew fattens up on crowberries, worms, and insect larvae, before flying south to the end of the continent, logging in close to 10,000 miles on the flyway.

Just about every ornithologist and biologist in the world believed the more unfortunate outcome: the last Northern Stilted Curlew had decades ago made its final annual migration north to south.

Samuel heard the pine needles crush before he saw the two figures ambling toward him. He expected to see more birders along the trail, at least a few of those semi-retired, Tilley-hat-wearing folks who check the rare birds database on the web nightly. But maybe the weather had kept them home. Or maybe, most just reasoned it was not worth the trip. A less rare, but much more plausible sighting, such as the Kirtland's warbler, or an accidental sighting of a species way out of its range, like the Cuban pewee in South Florida, would draw dozens in pursuit.

Here in these pines forty hours earlier, an amateur had spotted what he *thought* was the Northern Stilted Curlew. This same scenario happens often.

An excited birder could easily mistake the long bill, dark brow marking, and the strong, rapid wing beats of the white-bellied, stilted Whimbrel for that of the cream buff-bellied, and slightly smaller, Curlew. From a distance, it's also easy to confuse the long stilted legs of the Northern Stilted Curlew with those of the stilted sandpiper. The Curlew's delicate pinkish buff under the wing, the decurved bill, and its unique call would be the most distinguishing features.

"See anything?" he asked the couple.

"Nothing but a bunch of squirrels," the woman said.

The man wore pants and a Columbia rain slicker, a hunting-style cap, and a small hiking pack. The woman wore the standard, floppy Tilley hat, a thick fleece shirt, shorts with long socks above her old running sneakers. She toted binoculars and a Canon SLR around her neck.

"And a few Carolina wrens and one ruffled titmouse," the husband added. "It's been pretty quiet."

"They'll be out when the rain clears," Samuel said.

"If it clears," the man said.

They knew he was here for the Curlew like they were.

"We drove down from Connecticut," the woman said. They were die-hards, Samuel thought. "She was seen near here, not far, right?"

The sex of the possibly-observed Curlew in question has been unknown. If it was in fact a Curlew, it would be difficult to distinguish the sex—both sexes look very similar, only the female is slightly smaller, and an immature can be mistaken for a female. It would be very difficult to determine if it was a female, unless the bird was seen up close. Samuel had written down the notification from the online Rare Bird Database:

Reported Northern Stilted Curlew...unconfirmed sighting... at Darney Bluff National Preserve, four-and-a-half miles northeast of the main trailhead, directly north of the old hunting check-in station along a short loop trail. The bird was observed for thirty seconds before it flew in a north-north east direction.

"The report said five-and-a-half miles northeast of the main trailhead, directly north of the old hunting check-in station," Samuel said.

"We were out that far, near the check-in station," the husband said and looked up. "That thunder doesn't sound good."

So they had been there, Samuel thought. That didn't matter. If the Curlew was still in this pine bluff, it could be in the same area, but not the same exact location. After the rain, the Curlew would fly east towards the marsh and eventually back out over the Atlantic to its flyway. The bird was more than halfway to its wintering destination, and it wouldn't wait here while it had such a long way to go.

Scientists consider sightings of extremely rare species to be only hypotheses that require rigorous examination. A bird presumed by many to be extinct would be countered with disbelief, and scorn. For Samuel, a peculiar observation in the Everglades four years ago, combined with a list of other reports, formed his hypothesis that the species may not be extinct. There's a lot of space left from northern Canada to Argentina for a handful of birds to become nearly invisible. It may just be able to exist undetected by any of us.

Only true scientific endeavor could reject or accept his hypothesis.

***

He kneeled in the dark space, took the small tarp from his rucksack and folded it atop the layer of pine needles. He tilted the mug, sipping the last of the coffee, including the crunchy grind sediment the filter didn't catch. Some of it stayed on his tongue, grainy and bitter, before he swallowed it down. He put the empty thermos into one of the compartments before taking out the 200 mm long lens and clicking it onto his favorite camera, an older digital Nikon. The Nikon was a few inches bigger, and heavier than the newer models, and Samuel liked the sturdiness of it. He set the 300 mm lens on top of the pack where he could reach. The two plates of egg-and-bacon that he ate at the hotel would be wearing off soon. He took out two granola bars from the side compartment.

Waiting it out, leaning against the back of the old three-walled hunting station, he was grateful for the half-rotten, weathered structure that stood between him and the *ptttt plunk plunk* of the rain beginning to fall on the rusted roof.

He sat with his back against the shelter, his arms around his knees so only a few drops of the rain slanting down into the black soil splashed onto his boots. The wind came though in an unsteady whistle. It was high-pitched, silencing all other sounds, and then hesitant but rhythmic. Without the motion of the hike to keep him warm, the photographer of birds rubbed his hands together.

He ate one of the granola bars and sipped some water and listened to the wind. Out here, he felt all right, cold but dry and sure that he was where he was supposed to be. He did not know if the Curlew existed. No one did. But here, once the rain cleared, he would continue to look. That is what he could do, and it is what he would do once the rain letup, which he could tell it would by that lighter shade of gray, the wind less cold and heavy. There were many things he had second-guessed, and maybe some of them he had once considered faith. He thought of everything he really had faith in. Some people had faith in things they grew attached to, or could claim ownership over. That wasn't true faith, was it? Was faith the very thing that made us less reckless? He had a long time to think about religion, and he was still formulating his take on it, but he did have faith in God's judgment over man. And a judgment would come.

He did have faith in dreams, dreams that sank right down into the images and sounds of thought. He had faith in the memories of his dreams. The memory of his wife when she was disappearing in the hospital, and how she would smile in the middle of the pain when he walked in. That was some kind of faith she had. A friend had told him once that he could move on, try to meet someone new. His friend was only trying to help him.

Samuel thought about his son, how when he was just a boy, four or five, all he'd want to do is hide up in his closet and sketch giraffes.

"It isn't hiding," his wife Lorine had said to Samuel. "The boy is living. Look at how happy he is."

Samuel worried because his son could remove himself from the world the way his father could. Lorine would tell him it was okay, their son was a beautiful, extraordinary boy, he was thoughtful and liked to draw, and if that meant he was a little different, who cares if he would rather spend the day sitting by a lamp in his closet sketching while every other boy on the street rode their bicycles in a pack.

She loved Ry so much, and maybe she loved him more because the boy had this different look in his eyes, eyes deep green like the different shades of a forest mixed all together. She loved the boy fiercely. She kept him grounded, but through her respect for him, she also kept him from changing. Even before he could walk, she idolized him. It was her idea to encourage him to apply to the new arts charter high school, and the scholarship to college. The boy was always thinking about his drawings, and in many ways he was just like his old man, but Samuel worried because he knew it would be easier for the boy if he would imagine less and interact more.

And now, thirteen months after his wife's death, Samuel saw how his son was walking the way a young man would when he was detaching himself further from the world. He was walking like no one could see him. By detaching himself from the world he was inheriting, Samuel hoped that his son could stand it, at least get through all the rough parts.

***

He looked out, through the rain.

Once the clouds cleared, the pines would let squares of sunlight flow through. But now it was a pale darkness between blue and gray under the pines. The high-pitched *hak hak hak hak* came above the wind, from the east. He leaned outside the shelter to hear the peregrine falcon's calls coming from the top branches of a maple tree less than a hundred yards off. Moving quickly but being sure not to startle the falcon, Samuel placed the camera and tripod on the pine needles and adjusted the aperture to let more light in the lens. The falcon appeared through the viewfinder—the bluish brown feathers and the dark gray malar stripe and the broad wings tucked along his side. She was an immature, maybe a year old at the most. Samuel snapped a dozen photos—some with the falcon looking down, or straight ahead. And then a photo of the falcon staring sharply towards the shelter. She had decided the man and the clicking machine were too close, ascending from the branch with four swift sweeps of her white and slate-gray wings.

The photographer of birds kept his finger over the shutter, following flight with the camera lens, waiting for the shot of her with wings open, soaring directly above the tree. In a winter several years ago, under the grain towers in Superior, Wisconsin, Samuel had watched a peregrine, only slightly larger than this one, pursue and swoop down to strike a ring-necked pheasant in a spectacular dive, not more than thirty yards away. The speed and power of the continent's largest falcon is remarkable. Powerful and fast-flying, it is one of the most graceful of the birds of prey.

Feathers had exploded from that pheasant when the talons struck. The blast of feathers, the power of the collision, the deep black of the peregrine's eye. It was one of the photographs Samuel was most proud of.

***

Long after the peregrine had flown off, the rain stopped, but the gray lingered. There would be no sun this afternoon. He packed up the rucksack, leaving out the camera, which he slung across his neck.

He hiked north on the park service trail, past the maple the falcon had flown from. He looked up, and stopped every few yards to listen. It was his habit. His son said he always had his head in the clouds. He turned down the narrow singletrack east now. After a half-mile, he heard another call. But this stopped him in his tracks. It was a call he'd never heard before, a call from a bird in flight that he could not locate.

Samuel stopped and listened. He had been walking when he heard it, and he knew sounds heard while walking could be distorted. Please, let me hear it again, he thought. Please, fly this way. The only movement he made was inching his fingers to the Nikon, to feel that it was there. It was a sound that matched descriptions he had read, a sound that no one had ever recorded.

He did not hear the sound again. He listened, standing then sitting under the wrinkled trunk of a tall pine, looking up into the sky. He saw a bird in the distance, a good two hundred yards off, flying low behind the pines, and it was gone. He took his field journal and pen from his rucksack. With the journal to a new, unmarked page, he wrote his location as best as he could describe it, noting how far he was down the trail past the narrow creek bed and describing the pine taller than the other trees.

When he got to writing the sound, he found there was no exact language to describe it. It was a soft whistle—no not a whistle—that was the word that he remembered from reported accounts of the Northern Stilted Curlew. In 1949, after the species was already decimated from intense hunting and disappearing habitat, biologist Frank Kerrson saw a pair of Northern Stilted Curlews, and described their call as "a low tremulous whistle." Audubon, who had sketched the Curlew for his *Birds of America*, described the call as "a soft whistle."

Samuel scribbled and crossed out and then wrote:

Initially, it was like someone trying to whistle loudly but blowing air, a half-whistle. Like that, but three-noted, more musical. All sound broke off as quickly as it came. But I stopped in time to hear the call again, including the final note that was distorted when I first heard it. The bird called in series of threes in the same pitch, not more than three series, before movement, the last series of faint calls **tee-teeee-teeee**.

He did not hear the sound again.

He listened, looking up to the rain falling again, the gray lacking light. He listened for the bird to call again. An hour later, he headed back towards the trailhead, still listening.

Rain dripping off his hat low, he walked past the perfectly still fox looking out from his den of green. The man's boot steps were the only sound beside the rain falling on the pines.

CHAPTER TWO

Winter Beach, Florida

The water was almost still. There was no movement on the docks. A tarpon circled, its rolling body visible under the dim dock lights. This was where Samuel's son Ryan had come when the sadness could have broken him apart, and he had come when things just started to get a little better, when he had learned to live with the loneliness. That was not too long ago to forget, and it probably wouldn't ever be.

From the dock, the bay reminded him of a Highwaymen painting, with the soft blues of a Monet water scene. But he wasn't here to sketch that.

Ryan was trying to remember everything from that Tuesday afternoon, starting with her face as white as the paper.

After a minute, another truck passed.

Her hair a flat black, her eyes blue-green, mouthwash-clear. That is the best way to describe the color. He could paint it better than find words for it. The faded scar on her cheek, running from the lower edge of her eye down to her taunt cheekbone. The scar a fracture through time, the tiny marks left from the stitches. He would draw the scar last.

There's an old lighthouse on the hillside that overlooks the ocean. It doesn't shine a light anymore, but far out on rough seas, it sends a light for the young artist to see. She won't be smiling. Her eyes are all the expression there ever was. She'll be standing, looking out from the glass like she would watch the rain pouring down when she was a kid. She will be there looking out the glass from the lighthouse. It is a lighthouse that was built a long time ago, but had nothing inside.

Karia had her hands full when she came towards the door. She came towards the door and he closed the sketchpad and put his mug on top like it was a large coaster. She had her hands full, and pushed the door open with her foot, he remembers.

He saw the scar that was hard to see through the glass. Hank, the big dog under the retired engineer's table, looked up with alert ears as the girl walked out, and when Hank knew that the noise approaching was the girl, his tail started thumping against the brick pavers. The dog could smell her, the overlapping scents of handsoap, faint chocolate and cinnamon, coffee, the traces of sweat unmasked by perfume.

She walked up to Hank, and his tail thumped faster. The girl leaned down to pet him on the soft fur between his ears and gave the dog a biscuit from her pocket, which he took gently in his mouth and went back under the table to chew. The retired engineer smiled and thanked her. She smiled down at the dog, all black, with one white blaze. She walked over to another table to pick up the discarded mugs and plates from the afternoon crowd. As she bent down, her scar cracked into pieces.

If she saw that he was sketching her she'd probably think he was some kind of psycho, or just another guy who just wanted to sleep with her. Would she just walk to the next saucer she had to pick up? She would have to think he was a jerk, or an asshole, and she'd probably avoid him. Not that she spoke to him at all. It seemed like she didn't like most of the customers, unless you could count the dog as one. She wasn't mean though. It was as if she was in between being awake and being asleep all of the time, and she was trying to make sure not to jolt herself awake.

She had her hands full of the empty mugs and saucers and managed to open the door by cradling everything so she had three fingers free. She walked inside. Ryan watched her until the sun's reflection painted the glass, breaking his field of view. The dog watched her too, and put his head back down on the bricks.

***

He had this dream. This was four years ago, just before they drilled two tiny holes in his mother's skull to let the chemo treatment seep in. In the dream, it was early, early morning, still dark, and his mother went outside to get some fresh air. She walked around for a few minutes and came to a well. She looked down into the well, curious maybe about this well that was never there before. She carelessly fell in. Ryan's father ran outside, screaming her name, but the well wasn't there. There was no well anywhere. Ryan couldn't sleep after that because the dream would come back to him.

Not long after he had the dream for the first time, he had quit his Architect One job, the job that made his old college friends jealous, after just five months, to start working the early shift scrubbing boats and hauling around parts at the marina. He started coming to the café to sketch, on those afternoons when he wouldn't fall asleep from working in the sun. Some want to work behind the green-glass of the new buildings, and the older men at the marina wonder why he doesn't want to. The older men figured he'd go back soon enough. He kept on working. And in the afternoons he would draw. There was nothing good anymore, except that. He would sleep the nights he could, when the dream didn't come back to him, when he didn't wonder if she had fallen or jumped into the well. So he worked hard in the sun and in the afternoon he began building a tightly-constructed, impenetrable shelter— while those he had once been friends with talked about New Urbanism, the best entry-level jobs, and stock options.

CHAPTER THREE

The bones are thin, hollow inside, filled with oxygen, and supported with trusses that keep them strong. The wing bones are fused to other bones to brace together the moving parts in flight and landing. Look at the bones of a bird and, although all stretched out, they will match a mammal's skeleton. Side by side, compare those scientific sketches from college biology and see how the wings anatomically correspond exactly to each human bone from arm to the longest finger. But in birds, the bones are simplified, compacted so that the humerus, radius and metacarpals are welded into a single, pivoting elongated bone.

The muscles are different too, evolved for agile flight, aligned to control feathers independently. The respiratory system can propel some birds to an altitude of thirty-six thousand feet where no other animal could breathe without slipping directly into unconsciousness. Birds' lungs are anatomically very complex, funneling a crosscurrent of air and blood that allows them to exchange carbon dioxide for oxygen much faster than any mammal.

In some species, the bones are even lighter than in other birds, keeping their wing muscles from metabolizing more energy during long migratory flights. Inside the Northern Stilted Curlew, a warrior of long-distance flight, the bones must be lighter than its feathers. Audubon thought the Curlew's muscles used oxygen more efficiently than other birds, and he cited evidence that their lungs were proportionally bigger than other shorebirds and ducks.

The Kootenai of Idaho revered the Northern Stilted Curlew and considered its annual trek back north one of the first signs of spring. Young men would have to trap a Stilted Curlew and release it unharmed except for a plucked tail feather. The elders would tell stories of how the shorebird flew many, many miles over unfamiliar lands to warmer climates in the winter.

That was before the Stilted Curlew (*Numenius borealis phaeopus*) was slaughtered by the thousands both along its migration routes in North America and on its wintering grounds in South America. Also contributing to the species decline was the widespread conversion of northern prairie land to farms, and housing development along coastal migration stops. Since the 1950s, it has hovered near extinction.

***

By the time the morning light came through the window, the dark wood of the desk in Samuel's small office was covered with various guidebooks propped open with the empty mug or stapler or another book.

In the big guide, the *Audubon Master Guide to Birds of the Americas*, he flipped open to page 213 marked with a half Post-It stuck to the top of the page. There across the top of the page: Audubon's painting of the solitary Curlew wading in the marsh, and on the bottom a painting of the shorebird as it flew overhead, its Cinnamon-flash axillars and lining on the powerful wings, the long, wading legs tucked back in flight, and the dark eye and buff eyebrow strip painted in such fine detail it looked like a photo.

He is not a pretty bird, no handsome Cuban pewee or colorful roseate spoonbill. A strong flier, simple and utilitarian, ugly even. Stilt legs for the marsh, dull colors that blend into the prairie or marsh grass, the long bill for scooping up snails, strong wings and a steady flight. Samuel tilted the book closer. The webbed feet that can walk over rocks or through muck in the Curlew's open lake plain breeding grounds. The strong wings. Light bones.

Samuel reached for his mug of coffee that was now cold and with his other hand reached across the books to turn on the laptop, sending indigo and white illumination onto the room's walls. Soon Murphy 's '62 photos were up on the screen. Republished on the Wilson Ornithological Society's Web site, they were the last known photographs that exist of the Northern Stilted Curlew. Of the four photographs, only one was a clear capture.

In a brief published account, Murphy recounted the morning of May 2, 1962, in the backcountry of Wilson Sanford National Forest, Idaho, on a ridge overlooking the marsh shore of one of the Rilla Lakes. A spring storm had pushed in blustery wind and four days of constant rain, and May 2 was a dismal, soggy morning like the mornings before. Murphy wrote about how he rose from his tent tired and heavy with a nagging sinus cold. He tried to fix the makeshift kitchen tarp that had sunk low with rainwater, only to have the water pour out onto the opened coffee tin and food supplies. The rain was fraying his nerves and dampening his spirits, and Murphy planned to make the long hike back as soon as the rain let up.

The rain let up to a steady drizzle, and Murphy put the food and coffee out where it might dry eventually under the tarp. He was thinking of preparations he would have to make before he left camp, when he heard a distant call, and he looked up as two large birds came swooping up from the south. The birds were Northern Stilted Curlew, making their way back home, and landing down for a moment directly in front of Murphy. After seven thousand miles, the birds' precise flyway had taken them back to the glacial lakes of Northern Idaho.

Murphy's photos instantly drew attention, and for a short period there was renewed hope in the Northern Stilted Curlew. But a few months after his photos and report were published, a group who believed the Curlew had been long extinct disputed the authenticity of Murphy's photos. One well-known ornithologist and expert on shorebirds accused Murphy of staging the whole thing, planting stuffed specimens in a field for photographs.

In magazine articles and birders' chats, the dispute still continued many years after Murphy's death. One group argues that close study of the photos reveals that it was not a live bird. In two of the photos, one of the bird's stilted legs appears planted in the ground, and this group cites this foot as evidence that a stuffed bird was stuck firmly in the soil and then photographed from several different angles. The most damning evidence, however, was one color photo that looked eerily like an altered copy of a black and white photo. Some of those who say it's a fake, call into question Murphy's entire career.

Another group of birders and ornithologists say even if Murphy was guilty of doctoring a color photo, it does not make him guilty of entirely fabricating the photos. The most telling evidence for the believer's camp is the way the bird held his wing, folded tightly against the tail, in a way that shows he was alive, and not stuffed. It is impossible, they say, to duplicate this posture in a stuffed specimen. Either way, Murphy became the photographer who may have faked the photos of the Northern Stilted Curlew, and no one knows for sure.

***

The front door, which Samuel kept unlocked, swung open. The silence scattered.

"DAD."

"In here."

His son walked down the hallway.

"When did you get back?" his son asked.

"Yesterday."

"I called you three times."

"You did? Did you leave a voice mail?"

"You need to get a new phone."

"I should have made sure to check it." The father put the big guidebook up on the desk.

"I saw that South Carolina got hit with a bad storm."

"In the low country they just had rain."

"I've got to get to work," the son said.

"You want some coffee?"

"I should get going."

"Oh, before I forget, I found one of your old sketchpads when I was cleaning, it was under the bed."

"Where is it?"

"In your room, on the bed. Go up and get it," the father stood up now, "and I'll get you some coffee for the road. Are you growing your hair long?"

"No."

"It looks like it."

The son went down the hall, and up the stairs to his old room. He picked up the old sketchpad, pulling back the same cover he had so many times until there were almost no empty pages left.

CHAPTER FOUR

So his father was right, his hair is growing long, but he's not growing it long; he's needed a haircut for a while, and it's getting more and more blonde from the sun. He's okay with it. It feels good to wake up early and get to the water with only the old fishermen and the guys at the marina. He loves them for their simplicity. It feels good to work hard through the morning. He gets up early like the men who speak in Spanish over their coffee. They say hello and keep on talking when he gets to work, and the oldest one with the hardest lines on his face smiles softly at Ryan. But he can tell some of them wonder why he stays there, why he doesn't go back to work in one of those glass buildings.

***

He is going to use the greens and blues. Yes, the greens and the blues, lightly like shades of gray.

CHAPTER FIVE

September, the following year

Samuel sought answers in the glow of the laptop. It was dreary research.

Of those that no longer fly, the bones of the dispersive passenger pigeon would have probably been about equal in weight to the total weight of its feathers.

> Last seen in 1914. Cause of extinction: hunting on a massive scale.

The skeleton of the Chatham rail probably weighed slightly more.

> Last seen in 1900. Cause of extinction: destruction of habitat for sheep pasture.

The gentle-natured and unwary laughing owl, with its beautiful yellowish-brown and white plumage, had the large wing radius bones of an owl.

> Last specimen was found dead in 1914. Cause of extinction: predation by introduced predators such as cats, and widespread destruction of its habitat.

The tiny and drab dusky seaside sparrow had the delicate wing bones and tibia of the small Passeriformes. Field observations of banded dusky sparrows showed that the sparrow rarely traveled further than a mile or two in its lifetime. The last believed dusky sparrow, called "Orange Band," was left by himself in a Central Florida protected habitat, after what was believed to be the last five remaining male sparrows died. He became old for a sparrow and blind in one eye.

He died March 31, 1986. His delicate bones became a science specimen. Cause of extinction: Use of DOT pesticide starting in the 1940s, and habitat destruction to make way for Kennedy Center space shuttle compound.

He was still thinking about the lightness of birds when the e-mail came through.

-- **sent 9/20/2008 4:02 p.m. from bunting_birdworld@yahoo.com** --

Sam,

Found this Wilson Bulletin article by Randy Kerrson on the NSC. Never heard of this guy Kerrson but it's an intriguing account. I can see why you're becoming obsessed. I think this curlew may be a grail.

If you want to head south to take a look, we'll set it up. Whatever else you see we'll run. We haven't run a South America photo essay in a while. The vireo and tanager should be abundant this time of year (if you're lucky enough to get one standing still).

Keep an eye out for the American golden plover, it is the only species with nearly identical flyway as the NSC!

Just let me know if you're interested, I'll have Dom get in touch with you.

Renee

Managing Editor | *Bird World*

***

Nine days later, Ibera wetlands, Argentina

Samuel paddled the kayak towards the north side of the tree island, where the marsh grass looked the thinnest.

Most species of shorebird, such as the large and noisy willet or the small, lonely solitary sandpiper, have large, sweeping wintering ranges and expansive breeding grounds that stretch across Central and South America. But the Northern Stilted Curlew is particular about where it calls home.

Rainy season was still at least a month away, and the water was low, leaving exposed a bank of organic muck where the brown marsh water met shore, muck where the long-billed Curlew—if any were here in this vast, open marsh—would scour for the small snails that were a staple of its winter diet.

The Curlew calls specific patches of breeding and wintering ground its home. It follows an exact, pencil-thin flyway route south every September, driven south along this precise migratory flyway year after year. Observations and studies from John Audubon in 1827 to 1830, and later by the young and daring Smithsonian biologist Roderick Ross MacFarlane in 1850s, show the Curlew's precise habits. The shorebird splits its time between a tiny chuck of glacial lake marshland and the Argentine Ibera wetlands. Historically, the Curlew held two specific swatches of breeding ground, in the glacial lakes region of Northern Idaho and the border marshes of Canada. And the Curlew follows its exact flyway route to its same wintering ground in the Argentine wetlands.

That's why Samuel wanted to know the location of Randy Kerrson's sighting. According to Kerrson's account in the *Wilson Bulletin*, about four miles south, south-east from this tree island, the retired high school biology teacher had nearly collided his kayak into the juvenile, long-billed shorebird picking up small snails from the muck. The bird flew up noisily in surprise, almost into and then over Kerrson, and landing down in the marsh fifty yards back. That was the last plausible sighting of the rare and *presumably extinct* Northern Stilted Curlew.

It was late, with two hours left until sundown, and there wouldn't be much time to set up camp.

Samuel pulled the kayak up until it was on dry, firm sand. He hiked to the middle of the island, and there was the platform where he thought it would be. The University of Argentina biologists built it in the clearing just before the small strand of slash pines. The ground here was two feet higher than the water. It was good, dry grainy soil, covered in tiny acorns and pine needles from the scraggly oaks and the strand of pines.

The platform was about twelve feet by ten feet, built using at least several boatloads of lumber. It stands raised four-feet from the ground, six feet from water level. If left alone, alligators stay away from human activity, and the two Argentine alligator species, the broad-snouted caiman and the black caiman, wouldn't likely crawl this far from water anyway. The biologists must have been worried about the yarara, an aggressive and venomous snake that can grow twice as large as a water moccasin. Samuel had never seen a yarara, and he hoped not to.

He went back to the kayak, and he heard something by the water. He aimed the telephoto lens. Through the lens, he saw what looked like an overgrown fox, with extremely long, black legs and red fur and a black crest of fur across his shoulders. The fox froze, his long legs anchored in the muck, and turned to run off into the tall grass.

As Samuel brought the gear to the platform, he began to think of dinner. He planned lima beans and rice, for protein, and for the first night's luxury, a dessert, the fresh mango he bought at the market near the *posada*. After he had carried all the gear up to camp, and dragged the kayak further onto the island and turned it upside down so no Yararas would try to sleep in it, he took a gulp of water from the big thermos, one gulp though because he knew too much water circling in his stomach would make his hunger worse.

The man at the *posada* had suggested a guide, and Samuel took the sheet of paper with the scribbled name and phone number, but never called him.

The other photographers would stay in the *posada*, which was some twenty miles from the park, and hire a driver to come out very early in the morning and meet the guide. The guide would take the photographer out on his flats boat. There wasn't anything wrong with that, and the guide could get you quickly to where you wanted to go. But Samuel preferred to work alone if he could. He always believed that was the way to get out "into the field," to get as close to blending in to the wild lands as you could. And before the rainy season started in November, even one of those light Mavericks wouldn't have been able to get back this far into the marsh.

He set up his camp on the elevated platform, which took a little getting used to, and waited for the water to boil on the small propane burner. Sitting in front of the tiny first bubbles in the pot on the burner, he remembered the woman walking down the only dirt street that ran through the village.

The market was not far from the *posada* on the dirt street. The only other vehicle he saw besides his rental Jeep was a mud-splashed Four-runner with a dented bumper and KC lights, one of the drivers who would take the photographers or tourists to the preserve. The Four-runner chugged along slowly, a few boys rode bikes trying to race the truck. A farmer was making trips with his wheelbarrow piled full of fly-attracting manure.

Two women walked down the side of the dirt street with a small boy maybe four or five between them. The woman with the lighter, shy fox eyes and the long hair in a ponytail reminded him of Lorine, when she was a few years younger than thirty, and their son was about the same age as the boy. The woman wore a small, silver nose ring, and she took tiny steps so the tiny hand holding hers could keep up. Maybe it was the way his wife came to him as he tried to fall asleep in the quiet *posada* room. Maybe it was the woman's long hair on her lower back, or her shy eyes, or the way she let the boy feel like he was walking big steps. It was Lorine he was seeing.

It was her holding their son's tiny hand. She was bending down to tie their son's shoe lace, looking into their son's eyes, kissing him on the forehead, the boy smiling when her lips tenderly touched his skin.

***

Day Two

He awoke early, well before the sun began its reign over the day. The island was alive with the chorus of the songbirds and warblers. Before he had his breakfast of oatmeal and coffee, he could hear the loud rolling trill of the gray kingbird, the soft whispering call of a yellow-throated vireo, and the bubbling chirps of a bobolink.

Samuel drank his coffee and listened to a scarlet tanager somewhere close by singing his high-pitched song of *chip-churr, chip-churr, chip-churr, chip-churrrrr*. He looked up to try to glimpse the brilliant contrast of red and black, but he wasn't surprised when all he saw was the thick green leaves. Despite the male's vivid coloring, this tiny guy is difficult to observe because he will perch motionless for long periods of time, hidden deep in trees or bushes.

The morning sun painted the water a softer reflection of clouds and sky as he paddled out past where the water lilies grew by the hundreds, past the second island of trees, towards the eucalyptus strand that looked like feathers growing right up against the edge of the water.

A shadow approached amid the clouds and sky on the water, and Samuel looked up to the swallow-tailed kite flying above. As the kite flew overhead, it came into focus through the 300 mm telephoto. The striking black-and-white coloring, the white head and body and black wings and the black ribbon tail drifting, the hawk looked like a suited Maitre d' making sure the first night's accommodations were sufficient.

The hawk, with punctured lizard hanging in talons, came into focus through the telephoto lens. It angled, and flew towards the trees on the third in the chain of islands. Calling in a series of shrieks, the kite flew in a half circle above the feather-like eucalyptus and landed atop the tree. Looking through the lens as he focused it, Samuel now saw the nest on which the Swallow-tailed landed. A second kite was waiting in the nest, this one was most likely the adult female; the one with the lizard was the male. Two small fledglings with beaks open wide popped their heads up.

His finger kept the shutter release halfway depressed for that instant it took the camera to bring light into focus—the fledgling took the lizard tail in her beak—he then pressed the shutter down to hear the faint, crisp. The dad leaned down to give the other fledgling another piece of lizard—Samuel held the Nikon steady, feeling the click of the camera.

He clicked off another fifteen good shots. The small hawks ate the entire lizard, the adult saving the claws for himself and the mom to eat. He checked in the viewer, at least half were very good captures, before he put the camera back so it slung over his neck and rested against his side, which allowed him to paddle comfortably and be able to reach for the camera when he needed it. Slung like that he would be able to reach for it quickly again. He wanted to put some space between him and the nest so he wouldn't disturb the birds. With the warm, early morning light and the 300 mm lens, the fledglings had come out so clearly—even from nearly 200 yards away—their eager black eyes, the magnificent contrast of soft white and black plumage, and even the light tan chest coloration—cast in the copper morning light. After paddling along a little ways, he took a sip of the coffee. Still hot. The kite nest, along with the coffee in the stainless steel thermos nestled there on the kayak's plastic floor, had him feeling good about the trip so far.

He wouldn't allow this early-morning temporary success to fool him too much. He'd captured some good frames, but they weren't the shot he was out here for. And it was going to be a long day. But maybe that would be the best approach. Just keep your eyes open, he told himself, and who knows what will cross your lens. It has worked for you before. There was that time he spotted that tiny Cape Sable seaside sparrow when he was camping down on the southern tip of Everglades National Park. He remembered how he watched the sparrow for twenty minutes, trying to get one good shot. He was so focused on the sparrow that for a moment he didn't see another tiny bird right in front of him, six steps away, the warbler in a small scrub oak, perched weightlessly, swaying with the breeze.

The warbler didn't stay still for long. She flickered from branch to branch in the tree. She really was tiny. Smaller than half the size of a mockingbird. Smaller even than the tiny scarlet tanager. Her bill was small, the lower mandible paler, and her legs proportionately long and thin. Her soft notes flickered, as she sang *bzz-bzz-bzz-bzz*. Samuel thought he wouldn't be able to get a still photo of the gray and yellow flash dancing from branch to branch, but he steadied his breath and the Nikon. It was not until the bird flew off that he realized she was a Bachman's.

A Bachman's warbler. Right there in front of him. The rarest songbird native to North America.

Later he couldn't believe the photos he captured. Most of them were junk, except two great beautiful captures. Renee ran those two—his first publication of many in *Bird World*. The day after the magazine came out, *National Geographic* called Renee; they wanted to re-print one of the images, the first photo Samuel had taken of the warbler, if *Bird World* would give them permission to do so.

Because comparatively little is known about the Bachman's, the reasons for its decline are not clear. Samuel's photographs were among the eight photographed sightings recorded in the past 25 years. Bachman's warbler—a frustrating, exhilarating, and continuously pursued North American bird—had been the subject of cartoons, threatened litigation, and international cooperation, but of no detailed field study. Nearly extinct, this species has been written off before, only to reappear. Recently, only lone birds have been observed, scattered at remote, undeveloped preserves throughout the southeast.

Ten years after that afternoon in the glades, Renee, still his editor, was sending him out for something like the Bachman's. But even more unlikely.

He paddled.

Clouds moved.

Samuel had to be the only person right now hoping for the sight of a Northern Stilted Curlew. People didn't go out on a hike to find a passenger pigeon. They didn't go out to find a ghost. Despite the odds, they would try for that Bachman's warbler in Florida, or the really optimistic ones would go in search of an ivory-billed in the Arkansas bayou. Across their range, recent appearances of the old ivory-billed percolated, thus hope remained.

The clouds slid over the sun, until there was no light pouring down over the water, leaving only its muddy brown color.

No one was looking for the Northern Stilted Curlew anywhere. Every birder probably wished the Curlew existed in a small population undetected by humans. Several accidental, unconfirmed sightings over the past three decades didn't provide any scientific ornithological evidence. If anything the scarcity of the sightings, and the doubt that surrounded most of the events, does more to confirm the demise of the species.

Yes, he'd be the only one. The only one who believed enough to actually seek the Northern

Stilted Curlew, to try to photograph the Curlew. Renee had put the curlew in lowercase, was it by mistake, as she quickly typed, or did she see the curlew as something to dream about, rather than a tangible species that existed? It was a silly thought, but he remembered the lowercase c, for some reason.

His mood began to change like the clouds moving. So he tried to stop the movement of his thoughts, but they were set in motion, drifting like the clouds until they were in place blocking the sun.

***

Day Three

By eight thirty, the next morning, day three in the Ibera wetlands, the sun was unrelenting all over again, and it got hotter with each minute.

The kayak passed again through where the lilies grew by the hundreds, and this morning a big fish spooked, sending ripples through the lilies. He paddled towards the eucalyptus strand where he could see the mother swallow-tailed kite poised and looking down at the man on the kayak. An unsteady wind of eight or ten knots did nothing to disperse the sun's heat. The sun was reigning master over the land. Even as he paddled under the thin shade of an eucalyptus, he could smell the heat rising.

At the end of the day, Samuel fixed dinner early, canned tuna over noodles, with his "camping sauce," powdered cheese and garlic, and a side of dried banana slices.

All light vanished after the sun sank, and none of it returned with the new moon. Sitting on the camping platform with only the light from the small LED lantern, Samuel could feel the flatness of the land surrounding him.

He could feel the darkness.

A limpkin called, intermittent at first and then calling his persistent night song, and Samuel felt less alone. He went in the tent, and after a few minutes turned off the lantern.

The bird kept calling.

The following morning, the only man in two-hundred square miles would embark from the same place in the tall grass.

He would paddle out once again.

***

Day Four

In the language of the Argentine Indians, Ibera basically means "gleaming, glowing, shining water." This gleam comes from the sun reigning unimpeded down on this flat, open landscape that retains so much water. Samuel felt the sun intensifying by the time he went down to drag the kayak through the high grass. There was no sign of anything else moving except for the tiny mosquitoes that trailed him. Even the one caiman sunning itself did not move when Samuel dragged the kayak towards the water.

CHAPTER SIX
Winter Beach, Florida

"This is a neat town," Renee said as the waitress brought out her mocha drink. "Thank you," and then turned back to Samuel. "It's so much nicer than Miami."

"Yeah it's low key," he said. "It's a good home base."

"What did you mean when you mentioned journalism work?"

"For the Trib. Mostly feature photography. They've got me covering a college reunion this weekend."

"A college reunion. That's news?"

"It's their fiftieth, and they're going skydiving."

"I thought you despised newspaper photography?" the magazine editor asked.

"I don't despise it. And a fiftieth reunion in the air wouldn't be too bad. Not all fiftieth college reunions would be like that."

"I've got plenty of work for you."

"Okay. I was just trying to have something on the side, and I wanted to let you know," Samuel said.

"All right. So you read my last email about that senior biologist with Idaho Fish & Wildlife?"

"I'm not sure—not sure we should be going out for the Stilted Curlew. Not unless we want to be chasing a ghost."

"No, no, no, this biologist was saying there was a string of sightings at this one glacial lake way out in the middle of the national forest."

"That was twenty years ago," Samuel said.

"Fourteen. One of the largest American golden plover rockeries is in that area, and the Curlew, this biologist believes, is probably breeding within the plover population, which would make it difficult to record. And this lake is way back, it's in the forest, inaccessible by road, so a small population would be able to exist without—well, you know the routine. This biologist I spoke to said you would need to get a permit with the forest service, to camp at the lake. It'll be a four-day hike. If you want to go in there, we'll set it all up. Not until early spring, beginning to mid-March would be the time to go."

She had that kind of everything-is-great-in-the-field enthusiasm about her that reminded Samuel that she was trapped in an editorial office most of the day.

"So we've got a month," she said.

"I don't know."

"You're supposed to say 'Yes. Set it up, Renee.'"

"So I'm supposed to just hope to be in the right place at the right time."

"You should go."

Samuel didn't say anything. He circled his mug on the table.

"I knew you were doubting since Argentina. That's why I flew down. It's normal for a long-term project, something like this. I'll pay you to go, no stipulations. Just go, and I'll pay you three times as much as what the newspaper would pay to shoot ten of those reunions."

He took a sip of his coffee.

"All right. Why though? Why the Stilted Curlew?"

"Because I'm getting sentimental. Very sentimental, and I believed you when you told me what you heard in South Carolina. It's worth another shot."

"Okay."

"Oh and you might not want to book too many assignments with the paper. I spoke to Garnett yesterday. He was asking all about you."

"He was?"

"He wanted to know what kind of wildlife photographer you were. I told him you're one of the best."

"Thanks for lying on my behalf."

"And I sent him those Kite photos, from Ibera. That was some good work, some of your best work, Samuel. You're a wildlife photog, not a newspaperman."

CHAPTER SEVEN

Winter Beach, Florida

The northerners will say there are no seasons in South Florida. Depending on their inclinations, they'll sit outside the café and talk about how it's either one long hot, miserable summer, or one beautiful vacation season that they're going to miss as soon as they leave to drive back to Jersey.

But Ryan could feel those seasonal changes, and he came to love the subtle variations. Now in early March, the breeze was almost the same, except you could feel how it had lost its coolness, and smell how everything was about to bloom. The butterflies were awake, zooming around the bushes as he sat down at his table in front of the coffee shop. A big orange one fluttered upside down below a flower.

Joel, the other barista, stood where she would be, usually leaning against the counter in between the espresso machine and the register. He was yelling something about the Red Sox game. One of the regulars, a guy who worked at the architecture firm on Second Avenue, was saying this particular Red Sox pitcher was a choke artist, that the Red Sox were going to lose the next game with him on the mound. Jimmy Cliff came through the speakers louder than usual.

Joel asked Ryan how it was going and what would he would have. The barista filled the hot water for the tea while continuing his conversation about such and such pitcher and something about the team's manager.

All the noise couldn't dissipate the emptiness that filled the place without Karia there.

"Where's Karia?"

"She got the day off. Boss told her she had to take the day off. But she left this note for you."

***

Ryan bowed when she put the mug of tea in front of him. He realized as he bowed that he was trying to remain delicate, less tall, almost invisible in the place he had wanted to be. She looked out the window at the oncoming darkness. Her eyes moved from the window to his hands around the mug.

"Wish I could have a dog of my own, but it would be cruel to keep him in such a cramped space."

"You have Hank."

"He just loves me because I give him treats."

"No way."

Her hand on the counter was shaking.

"I'm wired," she said, and her eyes looked at him. "Had two cups of coffee this afternoon. I never have it after ten in the morning. And I stopped taking my meds."

"What meds?"

"Zoloft, Imipramine, Fluphenazine, whatever the cure of the month was."

Ryan held his hand around the mug and looked down.

"They're antidepressants, mostly," she said. "I told my shrink I didn't want to take them anymore, and he wrote me a new script, for this drug Luvox."

"So you're taking that?"

"It was the same thing. I was numb—I couldn't even hear the rain, a song of splashes on the roof and the gutter that I remember. The rain became just a perpetual thud. I just want to feel... I'm rambling now."

"You're not rambling. How long ago did you stop taking it?"

"Three days."

He reached over, and this surprised him even, he took hold of her hand. It was still shaking. She retreated. And then put her hand back so she could run her fingers across the smooth, darker scar on his smallest knuckle.

CHAPTER EIGHT

Early Autumn
Solitudo County, Idaho

Past midnight it dropped back down into the thirties, and in the morning, when Thomas woke with the arrival of the sun as he did every morning, he could see the mist through the glass, spread across the horizon like an unraveled thread of white yarn.

The shepherd husky mutt was asleep, curled up between his legs. Japhy usually slept on a thick blanket at the foot of the bed, but on the cold nights he would curl up on the bed between Thomas's legs or beside him. It was survival instinct, something both man and dog were grateful for. Even if Thomas stoked the wood furnace before he went to bed, by early morning coldness would fill the small bedroom.

As Thomas put his clothes over his long johns, the dog lay on the bed, stretched out, watching Thomas lazily before shutting his eyes. He had reached that age when dogs like to sleep in later than their human counterparts.

Thomas went to the kitchen and filled a pot with water for tea. He put the pot on the furnace and turned on the radio to the NPR station, which came in mostly clear.

There was news of a suicide bomber in Iraq and flooding in the southeast. Another Ponzi schemer was in jail. The unemployment rate upticked to 9.1 percent after two months of holding steady. Average hourly earnings were down 11 percent from two years ago. Then came the regional news update.

The journalist reported on the latest with the rush to drill wells into the shale of recently-discovered natural gas in Solitudo County.

Houston-based Centur Corp. began clearing a site for a third exploratory drill on cattle baron Harold S. Canson's property bordering the Wilson Sanford National Forest, approximately five miles north of Wolf River.

Meanwhile proponents who continue to lobby to open federal lands, including Wilson Sanford National Forest, to the process of natural gas extraction known as hydrofracking won a victory in court Friday. An Idaho Circuit Court judge struck down the request for an injunction against all hydrofracking on and within a mile of federally-protected lands. The recently-formed conservation group Protect Our Wild Lands filed the request for an injunction against the drilling two months ago. Stephen Williams, a lawyer with the group, was lead counsel for the injunctive suit.

"It's becoming painfully clear that natural-gas hydrofracking wreaks havoc on water wells and our rivers, streams, and lakes," Williams said. "Without further regulation, allowing such activity within the National Forest and a stone's throw from the federally-protected Wolf River and its tributaries will have irreversible impacts. We are currently requesting that all drilling and surveying work within one mile of Wilson Sanford Forest be suspended until the EPA provides a regulatory framework for such drilling. Further litigation is forthcoming."

Governor Scottson has continued to publically voice support for natural gas drilling on certain Federally-Protected Idaho lands. In a recent interview, Scottson said drilling would revive the state's economy, and for that reason he plans to reverse a moratorium prohibiting all drilling on the state's protected lands.

Scottson painted recent media reports of environmental concerns as exaggerated and quoted estimates that local drilling could create more than eight thousand high-tech jobs and net two billion dollars in revenue for the state in five years. Scottson spoke to WLRN Tuesday. "Various studies have found no credible threat to drinking water from hydrofracking. People are looking for a problem that doesn't exist. And I'll promise this. I'm going to stick up for this industry because this is a clean energy source that is going to employ thousands of people here."

Several national environmental groups say using natural gas will help slow climate change because it burns more cleanly than coal and oil. And Scottson is joined by local lawmakers who hail the gas-drilling as a source of jobs. They also see it as a way to wean the United States from its dependency on other countries for oil.

But the relatively new drilling method — known as high-volume horizontal hydraulic fracturing, or hydrofracking — carries significant environmental risks. It involves injecting huge amounts of water, mixed with sand and chemicals, at high pressures to break up rock formations and release the gas.

Opponents say the resulting wastewater contaminates nearby drinking wells and watersheds.

Thomas snapped off the radio.

Outside, pale blueness poured down upon the white mist.

It had been inevitable for sometime. Test drilling meant drilling when they found natural gas like they did. That pocket of natural gas was worth ten to twelve billion, he'd heard. That was enough to drive men to do anything. And they wouldn't be satisfied now until they've torn up these mountains, just like the timber company cleared the forests two counties south, acre by acre until they could claim every virgin growth western white pine that had grown through the dark soil. Just like these same men did with the oilrigs off the coast of Louisiana before the big spill.

Thomas would have to call Williams Monday, and find out when Protect Our Wild Lands would file the appeal. He met Williams three years earlier at one of the public hearings on the oil leases. They were walking out of the town hall annex at the same time, and Williams, still holding his hat in his hand, said they were all in for a fight. Thomas told him everything would probably come down to a fight between the lawyers. "I'll go down swinging on this one," Williams had said. Thomas remembered that.

***

Thomas sat on the tailgate of his forest service Dodge and drank from the mug of coffee. He had saved the last half of it for Highline Ridge, and now he didn't mind the tiny grayish bug floating on the surface, making small ripples in the coffee. It wouldn't be the first tiny unidentified bug swallowed by man. The shepherd-husky mutt stood on the tailgate, his ears up, nose poised, sniffing all the scents in the wind.

It wouldn't stay above forty degrees much longer, Thomas thought. The sun was bright, but even with the thick flannel over his uniform, he could feel that late autumn wind. He had to check on the traps on the ridge that Fish & Wildlife set up as part of their program to trap wolverines and collar them with GPS trackers. Traps were the only way to catch a wolverine because they wouldn't come within ten miles of humans. The traps on the ridge, which were Thomas's responsibility, had been empty for the past year, but they had to be checked every week. If he found anything, Fish & Wildlife would come out and tranquilize the animal, examine the wolverine in the field, and fit them with the GPS collar. A few years ago Thomas helped collar W-52, a scrawny, malnourished five-month-old kit that was separated from his mother after the mom probably died in a fight with another adult. The kit was helpless and exhausted, letting the men insert the hydration needle before he was fully sedated.

He drank the last of the coffee.

"You ready to do this?"

As the shepherd-husky mutt would reply to all questions posed, he was alert and ready. The answer was yes, and the dog jumped down from the tailgate when Thomas stood up.

They set out on the trail that cut across the open mountain prairie of tall, faded brown wild grass towards the edge of ridge. It was a good, mostly flat trail, with the clearest views over the western half of the national forest. This is the high country, a wild, vast land, ragged. The country was taking on the hues of winter.

It's not one of the parks packed with adventurous eco-tourists. It's not the snow-covered peaks of the postcards or the brilliant reds of Grand Canyon, and there ain't no backcountry tram tours coming through, ferried up from resorts or hotels. He might see a few lone hikers, and come December, he'll go days without seeing anyone. There isn't even a hotel for ninety miles. There is one ski resort, but those tourists spend most of their time in the resort. There are two motels just outside the county line, ninety-five miles south. There isn't a road for thirty miles in any direction except the old logging trails and fire roads. It's a big square on the map, a country left aside.

The wind smelled like clean running water, the pine tops stood blue to the west, frozen in thin frost and untouched yet by the white sunlight.

Beyond that the land folded down into Big Fern Gulch, the waters of Wolf River steady at the bottom. The ferns pale amber like the grass, and everything was that dull shade of gray or brown except the tops of the half-barren lodgepole pines and the burned-out yellow of the aspens on the other side of the gulch.

Behind the man and his dog, to the east, the twin hills rose up as if the land had grown over two sleeping giants, and further to the east the jagged-cut, snow-covered mountain peaks that stood above the land.

The first trap was empty.

"Let's take the loop," he said aloud, which Japhy interpreted as another question, to which the dog replied by trotting ahead. The full loop of singletrack trail was about thirteen miles. They headed north, further across the prairie, open and gray, and cold in the wind.

On the northern edge, they hiked through the strand of ten-year-old lodgepole pines, the thin, half-barren trees leaning over the trail where they had cleared the forest here two springs after Thomas first hiked this ridge. Someone always saw this land as a forest to be harvested, and they came with the machinery of their time to try to get as much as they could. Covered in frost, the young lodgepoles grew where the old ones crashed down like thunder. Then the strand of the big trees came up suddenly, shading the trail. These lodgepole pines, and a few taller western white pines, grew four and five times as tall as the young trees. These were the one left, by chance, from the blades of the chainsaws before the logging men moved on.

Standing under the windless shadow of one tall white pine, Thomas looked north at the forest left by chance from the saws and the dozers.

The first time he had hiked Highline Ridge, out here a good two thousand miles from everything he had known, the sun had broken through the clouds, but he could only see small squares of light through the pines. That first time he had hiked Highline Ridge twelve years ago, his rucksack had been packed to the brim for seven days of camping.

Strapped to the pack, had been the old sleeping bag and that canvas Army tent his uncle gave him before he left. He remembered stopping near here under a white pine, taller than this one even, taller than anything he had seen in New England. That pine was the tallest tree he'd seen, the thick, wrinkled trunk reaching upwards, leaning as if the wind had tilted the tree after all these years. Dogwood grew up along the tree. There was no undergrowth in the cool shade beneath the tree except for a patch of deer fern. Thomas didn't know then that unlike many other pines, the western white pine is native only to the most northern reaches of the upper Rockies and is the state tree of Idaho. He only knew the tree's vast size as he'd sat below it. He didn't know the white pine faced deadly threats such as the invasive white pine Rust Blister or widespread logging that sawed-down the old growths throughout Idaho in the last twenty years. He would never have guessed that he soon would be involved in the effort to save the western white pine.

Two days later, the small posted sign in the ranger station stopped Thomas before he left to head back home. The sign called for temporary summer help clearing service roads in the park. He walked into the ranger station.

***

Now Thomas could see ahead to where the puffs of clouds drifted down and nearly touched the twin mountains, off to his right. The trail took them further into the white pines and the tall lodgepoles that had never been logged, each canopy a layer over the other, as high as fifteen stories in some places. The sun made no impression here, and it was cold for October even.

The dog led the way with his muzzle in the pine needles. He stopped and sniffed around a track, big wolf prints, that intersected their paths, and Thomas kneeled down to take a look.

The wolf prints were the size of his hand.

The trail cut along the western edge of the ridge here, right above the wide deer ferns covering the gulch, the ferns an amber brown, and further down, Wolf River flowed its course.

The trail went up into the forest. Old growth. Some of the trees as old as four hundred years, untouched, the southern edge of the old forest that extended north up to Rilla Lakes.

***

The hike felt good, eight or so miles now from the truck, and it was cold under the pines, but he knew the sun would pour down bright in the prairie and he'd need to pull his hat low to keep the sun from hurting his eyes.

He hiked through the pines. He knew those cold January days would be coming soon. He felt it in the wind. He tried not to think about what they said on the radio, tried not to think about how many drills will bore into the earth by next autumn. But he did think about it. He could see the giant drill bits turning through soil and rock. He saw the bits turning with all their mechanical ferocity, saw them drilling into the forest where he stood. The chemical-laden water pumping down into the soil to break through the shale, and the lakes of wastewater left over every day from the water forced into the ground.

He tried to empty the image from his mind. When he got back to the truck, he sat for a minute before he drove the two-rutted forest service trail with the combination of cold air from the half-open windows and the worn comfort of the old flannel he wore. The shepherd-husky mutt leaned against the door panel with his muzzle out the window. Thomas felt the wind.

CHAPTER NINE

Spring
Solitudo County, Idaho

The old logging bridge was no more than ten feet wide and built of heavy, splintering timber. It was blocked by another row of three large boulders that Samuel walked between. Hammocks of red cedars grew upstream along the river, with one of the tallest tree's rooted in the shallow water on the eastern shore, its reflection in the river. Samuel envisioned the landscape shot he could have taken if he had brought the tripod and wide lens. Even without the tripod, maybe he could get a shot on the way back. It would be best in the indirect, soft light of dusk.

There were only two bridges over the river. Both were thin-dotted lines on the topographical map. The other one also was a narrow wooden bridge, that one built by the forest service, nearly thirty miles south at Overlook Pass.

He took the old two-rutted logging trail another half mile until it faded into tall grass between the needle-straight forests of second growth lodgepole pines. A mile further, the footpath went up between two lodgepoles.

After the first cutback in the trail he heard a loud bang like dynamite in the distance. The ground vibrated. After thirty seconds another loud bang echoed.

The bang came again, directly to the east, followed by a sound more muffled, a constant, clanging, droning noise. There was more banging, like someone was slapping thick chains against metal.

After he had hiked through the morning, the river was far behind him.

Samuel carefully lowered his pack when nine hours later he reached the foot of the first ridge. The back of his shirt and the stripes from where the straps had pulled into his shoulders were covered in sweat. Down on a knee he took out the GPS from his pack, just to be sure.

***

Samuel camped the second night on the ridge from where he could see the southern edge of the lake. Still an eleven-mile hike to go. It was large even for this land, and purple in the dusk light. To the west, he could see the marshy tributary where the lake's waters fed into Wolf River.

On the level ground he swept aside the acorns and tiny branches as best he could, and he set up the tent. It was a small and low tent and tidy with his pack and the camera gear stowed in the corner.

The tall western white pines were behind him, and two stout spruces framed his view looking out from the camp. He watched a tiny grosbeak flickering and a minute later a rough-legged hawk gliding past. He looked at his watch, it was ten after six. Immense beauty and solitude surrounded him, but the grosbeak, now whistling *whee-you* a few pines away made him happy, and he hoped the bird would stay there whistling for a little bit. The grosbeak flew up to a higher branch. The bird burned a tiny flare with its copper-orange flanks and yellow underwing glowing in the forest's blue-gray dusk light, before it jumped off in flight to another tree.

Samuel had came here, the narrow trail that eventually lead to Rilla Lakes, seeking the Northern Stilted Curlew, the bird revered by the old tribe of the Kootenai of Idaho, the elders once telling stories of how every spring the shorebird flew north many long miles over unfamiliar lands to get back home.

That was before, as the Audubon guidebook put it,

"...commercial hunters slaughtered the Stilted Curlew (*Numenius borealis phaeopus*) by the thousands, both along its migration routes in North America and on its wintering grounds in South America. The widespread conversion of northern prairie land to farms, and housing development along coastal migration stops also contributed to the species' decline. Since the 1950s, it has hovered near extinction."

The lake may be the last breeding ground for the long-billed shorebird that Samuel had been seeking. By the white glow of the small camp lantern, the photographer of birds looked down at the topo map. Tracing his route with a finger, Samuel saw that the first three miles of the next day's hike continued to climb a thousand feet a mile, until the land descended gradually to the lake. The cumulative elevation change was about 2.2 miles up.

***

He slept well for eight good hours, and as he sat on the edge of the tent in the early morning and put on his boots, he thought about the hike ahead. It takes three days of good hiking to get to the lake. Samuel would get there two hours or so before sundown, just in time to set up for dinner, a luxurious dinner of rice and beans and the dried fish, and the orange he has saved for dessert. That was the plan, but first he walked down to the narrow brook below camp.

He knelt by the brook to fill the jug with the numbingly cold snow water. He packed up the camp as the water boiled for his coffee and oatmeal, and he boiled another pot and poured the disinfected water into the thermo. Once his boots were back on the trail, he turned the Nikon on, and slung the camera around his neck and off to the side so it hung balanced by his ribs, where he could reach it quickly.

The lake was on the other side of the pine forest, cradled on a shelf between two mountain crests. The lake called Rilla Four Lakes looks like four separate water bodies, but it is really one large glacial formation.

Samuel had the smaller Nikon and the 300 mm lens, a setup that was a few pounds lighter than his other digital Nikon with the longer telephoto. The sky showed in smaller patches, and soon it disappeared under the canopy of western white pines and ponderosas. After cutting through the forested foothill, the narrow trail went up in switchbacks, and Samuel looked down for snakes before stepping over the branches that had been knocked down in a windstorm. It was hard to tell how high the canopy of western white pines stood, but it was high—the pines growing straight up through the slanted earth.

***

The pinecones of the white pines here were twice as big as the ones on the trees near his camp on the first night, back on the edge of open prairie and mountain forest.

He hiked at a good cadence. He had slept through most of the night, but he was feeling the lumbar intrusion from sleeping on the hard ground. This was no east coast forest. The pale sun became paler, and dissipated into the air before reaching the bed of pine needles spread on the ground.

Awe and solitude are the two most immense points of view, and here they were the same. He kept going, grateful for the warm ache in his legs, and his back feeling a little less sore, but he knew the loneliness could come at any moment with the blowing and falling, eerie, unimpeded rhythm of the wind, so Samuel began to sing a James Taylor song about dogs and glasses of beer in the cowboy's dreams, sang it in his head, silently, because he didn't want to add noise to the environment other than the soft crush of the pine needles under his boots.

He would have liked to have been able to tell Lorine about this forest. He would have liked to tell her about these big old growth trees and this quietness except the wind, how you feel smaller and smaller the further you hike. Everything he would do and see, he knew when he was out in the field, that he would tell his wife, he would be anxious until he told her about his trip. It was the single entry point back to the other world that he looked forward to, and he would never get used to not having that first dinner back, his stories slightly exaggerated from the two glasses of wine. He wouldn't get used to her absence.

***

A dog barked aggressively, and came running down the trail. Samuel stopped. He heard a voice calling for the dog, and saw a tall figure catch up to the shepherd. As the man and dog came closer, the park ranger had a face that matched all six-foot-five of him, a big face with sharp lines that came down to a square chin, his eyes too far apart, just slightly askew, and a large forehead under his hat. His thick eyebrows matched his dark, untrimmed beard. With his worn panama hat, he looked a little more like a farmer than a ranger.

"Hi," the ranger said, and the dog, a shepherd husky mix, stood by him, keeping his eyes on the stranger, snarling an occasional deep bark-growl.

"Man, you've come all the way up," The ranger took off his hat. "What're you photographing?"

"Birds."

"Just saw a beautiful rough-legged hawk," the ranger said, and he smiled a half smile-grin. "He's a resident up here."

"You know anything about the Northern Stilted Curlew?"

"No, wait. Curlew—I heard one of the Fish & Wildlife biologists talking about it. A big, kind of ugly shorebird. It's listed as extinct, or a rare species in Idaho?"

"No one is sure."

"Well, friend, I'm not an expert on it—be sure to stow food supplies good, and you might want to burn your food after cooking," the ranger said. "Japhy pointed out two big grizzles just up north," the ranger looked north, "before you cross over into the conservation area. They were big fellows, about four-feet tall on all fours."

"Will do."

"My name's Thomas," The ranger said.

"Samuel."

"This is Japhy. He's a little suspicious of new people. We didn't figure we'd see anyone up this way anyhow."

"Hey, pup," the photographer of birds said to the dog that had seen a squirrel or rabbit in the woods and wasn't so concerned with Samuel anymore. "Back at the river, there was this loud banging noise—"

"At the bridge?"

"Yeah, sounded like dynamite," Samuel said.

"They're testing for gas. Wasn't dynamite. They use something like a giant hammer on a truck to send down seismic waves to test where there are pockets thousands of feet down under the surface."

"Can they even drill here? On National Forest land?"

The forest ranger didn't say anything at first. He just stood there looking down, and he dug his boot into the earth.

"Yeah. It's looking like that," he said after some time. "There's a pocket of natural gas under here big enough to make men do anything."

He looked at the ground. Then he put his hat on, and before he turned to hike south towards where the trail switched under the white pines, he reminded the photographer to remember to stow his food good, and to be sure to check in at the ranger station when he returned.

***

Samuel hiked, slowly, and at a good cadence through the last of the pines and into the edge of open prairie. It was getting dark, and he would set up camp soon.

CHAPTER TEN

By the fourth morning, Samuel had crossed forty hard miles, through three distinct ecotones, an elevation gain of four-thousand feet, and he had four more miles to go. The foothills of the lower Selkirks were behind him, rising up almost directly above, and the wide glacial lake ridge opened to the north.

He had those last few miles to go. But here Samuel could see the place he'd read about and seen photos of. A sun-lit speck of a hawk glided above the closest lake, circling low in the light wind gusts. The hawk was hunting, drifting in the wind and for a moment even appearing to fly backward along the shore. After the tall white pines and the cold forest of the giant cedars, and then the smaller cedars and pines, and the maple hammock, the lake plain was astonishing. Wide open and light and flat, it was the opposite of the forested lands Samuel had just hiked.

The grosbeak he saw earlier was a sign that many of the passerine migrants would be arriving, and the Merlin he heard would be one of the falcons to migrate north. By this time of year, the Curlews might have also made their way back home. So here the photographer was. Hiking north still along the trail that cut below the mountains and further towards the glacial lake plain.

There along the border of the lake, south of the marsh grass, Samuel could see the open field of crowberry where Murphy had sighted the Curlew and took the last undisputed photograph of the species.

A bird's heart is large, powerful, and of the same basic design as that of a mammal. It is a four-chambered structure of two pumps operating side by side. One two-chambered pump receives oxygen-rich blood from the lungs and pumps it out to the waiting tissues. The other pump receives oxygen-poor blood from the tissues and pumps it into the lungs. This separation of the two kinds of blood is different from a mammal, making a bird's circulatory system, like its respiratory system, well equipped to handle the rigors of flight. Because of the efficiency of the bird's respiratory system, the ratio of breaths to heartbeats can be quite low. All mammals take about one breath for every four and one-half heartbeats, a bird breathes about once every ten heartbeats.

Samuel thought about what the drilling would mean for the Northern Stilted Curlew—if the Curlew still existed in a small population struggling to survive. The lake plain was one of the last marshlands along the Curlew's northern flyway undisturbed by farmland, roads, or other developments. This marsh has remained inaccessible to even ATVs or snowmobiles in the winter, and it is one of the last homes to the crowberry—a once abundant fruit tree that the Curlew relies on as a main staple. The crowberry has been ripped up to clear way for farmlands throughout the Midwest and Northwestern states.

It is unclear why the stilted Curlew relies on the crowberries, and why the fields of crowberries surrounding Rilla Lakes, but Samuel read that one theory is because the acidity is lower than is typically encountered in forest berries, and benzene acids are almost absent, making it an edible staple for shorebirds such as the Curlew. This purple pebble-size fruit is especially vital when the Curlews just arrive after the five-thousand mile spring migration north. The fruit begins to ripen in late winter, and by spring many of the berries have fallen to the ground.

CHAPTER ELEVEN

Solitudo County, Idaho

The dog leaned against the door panel with his muzzle out the window.

A little ways past where the forest service road turned from dirt double-track back to asphalt, south of the old logging bridge, Thomas saw the Fish & Wildlife Suburban, and he pulled off to the side of the road and stopped.

"Hey," she said.

"Hey, Tift."

She got out of the suburban and walked around to the truck. She had cut her hair short.

"Hey Japh. How's my handsome boy." The dog was leaning out the window against her and licking her arm.

"I just checked the traps up here," Thomas said.

"They aren't going near them because they can smell us," she said. "They pick up our scent around the traps."

"I was thinking about that. Well, they ain't going to come up here anyhow now, not with all that noise. They can probably hear it from Sumter Mountain."

"Probably. Did you hear the radio yesterday?"

"Yeah," Thomas said. "I'm going to meet Williams tomorrow."

"You are?"

"Yeah."

"You think that's a good idea. I mean getting involved with—

"We're all involved. Whether we want to be or not."

"I didn't mean it that way."

"I'm just going to see him."

"Okay."

"I promise I won't chain myself to any bulldozers."

"Well, when it comes to the forest, I can see you doing that."

"I'll leave all chains, tree spikes, monkey wrenches and various protest equipment home." He grinned.

"Good idea. Seriously. Are you going to find out when the appeal hearing is?"

"I'll let you know."

"I've got to get back to lab."

"Did everything go Okay?"

"It's official."

"You all right?"

"Yeah I think so. I do."

"You're better off."

"Thanks Thomas. Oh I wanted to tell you. We tracked W-52 up in Jasper National Park."

"Calgary?"

"Yup. And he covered an average of eighteen miles a day on the trip. Over the Rockies."

"He's a trekker. I'm glad the little guy is doing well."

"Hopefully, he could breed up there starting next spring. I'm going to call Canadian Wildlife so they can track him."

"Good. Well you better get going. See you soon."

She gave the big dog a pet, and told Thomas they'll have to catch up soon, and she walked back to the Suburban.

***

A few miles down the road, the dog's ears bent back when the big rig came around the corner. The driver downshifted when he saw the forest service truck. The weighed-down rig had Centur Corp. painted on the door in dark brown letters, a pile of pipes and a drill bit the size of a small car cabled down in the bed.

It was headed to Canson's property, the tattooed driver looking straight ahead out the rig's streaked windshield as he passed Thomas.

That night, Thomas lay half-awake trying to sleep. The gleam of the moon dripped through the window, leaving its reflection on the thick wool blanket. He kept seeing a train of the trucks with the dark brown letters on the door. Unsure if it was real or something that he'd been told would happen soon—until he remembered the tattooed driver looking straight ahead and the black smoke from the rig's smokestack. He lay half-awake, his fear and anger mixed the way the moonlight mixed with the darkness.

CHAPTER TWELVE

Winter Beach, Florida

Her hand submerged slowly, becoming complete numbness. Karia filled the bath with the hottest water, glad that the water heater was working this morning.

She sat on the shelf of the tub and considered doing the same with her toes. If she let the cooler water run, the water would lose the heat that mattered so much, so she sat on the shelf for a minute, pouring in some of the bath crystals her aunt had given her as a gift at some point. The smell of lavender and something else potpourri rose up with the steam. It was almost too hot. She lowered in her toes, followed by her left foot. Numbness spread. Once she got down into the water past the top of her foot, or her ankle maybe, she knew she would be able to lower the rest of her body. Submerged up to her belly, it can be so quiet in the bathroom, she thought, with only the sound of faint splashes echoing. It must be the tiles and thick walls that make it so quiet.

She thought of his hands holding the coffee mug, his hands sketching. She wanted his hands to run down her cheek. She hadn't thought of a man like that since she was sixteen, before it happened. She wanted to reach out and feel the web of veins on the back of his hand.

She didn't realize she had stored the image of his knuckles and the web of veins on his hand. Knuckles protruded, the middle one a rock under the thin flesh. The smooth, darker skin on the smallest knuckle. Did he burst the flesh at work? Did he punch something, someone? His nails uneven, chipped away. The surface where the pencil would cradle between the thumb and index finger when he sketched. Sometimes it was the thumb and middle or thumb and little finger. Each position a different intensity of shade on the paper.

She held her hand. It wasn't his, but it had to do. She guided her hand along her side along the rib bones under tight flesh and down to the hip bone line.

CHAPTER THIRTEEN

Solitudo County, Idaho

Back up in Wilson Sanford National Forest for the second spring, Samuel sang the same song about dogs and glasses of beer in the cowboy's dreams, sang it in his head, silently.

The sun sinking in the west and the full white-gray moon floating in the east, he went down to the creek below his camp.

The trees blocked the wind but he could hear it smacking the top of the branches, which bent away from the westerly wind and swayed back when the wind let up. There was no sound except the wind through the trees, and soon the rush of the brook. This forest was dark and cold in the shade before he got to the brook and he could feel the warm sun.

Beside the creek he heard a high-pitched whistle, *klee klee klee kleeee*, and looked up. The kestrel stared down at the man. This falcon is sometimes referred to as the "Sparrow Hawk" or "Grasshopper Hawk," but its wonderful mix of brown, bluish-gray, black, and cream white deserves a more thoughtful nickname, Samuel thought. He had learned that the bird is sometimes called the "Sparrow Hawk" because, in the past, it was thought that kestrels primarily preyed upon sparrows, but that was before research indicated otherwise.

"Don't worry, I'm just here to get some water," the man said softly to the slender and colorful falcon that was his favorite bird of prey to watch.

But the falcon called a series of higher-pitched sounds as she stood on the edge of the branch, her underwing golden brown and cream, black patches speckled across, wings, tail feathers fanned for liftoff. The falcon soared away, and Samuel sat on the broken shale and began to fill the thermos.

Sitting on the rock beside the creek, he saw something flash in the water about five yards downstream—a blotch of silver. The fish floated above the shallow edge of the broken shale river bottom, dead in the water, its gut bloated like a balloon. There were four more dead fish on the shore.

The one floating in the water had the red-orange color slash below the jaw of the fine-spotted cutthroat trout, that species of trout that once flourished in mountain waters. A small, declining population of cutthroat survive in a few rivers and lakes here. Samuel had learned a long time ago that the species is considered an indicator of water quality. They can only take in oxygen from very clean, pristine, and cold waters. They need this clean, colder water to circulate oxygen, while the closely related rainbows can survive in much less clean waters. The Cutthroat would be the first ones to die off from the poison slowly trickling into the river. In the news, they said how natural gas was the new energy for this country, how it burned cleaner than coal or oil. They didn't talk about all the chemicals pumped into the ground and the carbons seeping back up from the rock strata through thousands of vertical cracks once the machines start extracting gas. They didn't talk about dead fish.

Samuel knew there would be more, and the fish wouldn't be the only ones.

He thought about the lightness of birds.

***

He packed up camp and hiked further. In the forest several miles north-northwest of the river he heard an assortment of warbler calls, and he started pishing to see what birds he could call to the area. Calling off the low, repetitive clicks, Samuel attracted a curious Virginia warbler and a blackpoll warbler circling in to land on a branch in the low brush. Then a chickadee came by to see what was happening. And the handsome magnolia warbler that Samuel tried to capture as the warbler foraged a few moments earlier. The black, yellow, and white warbler contrasted sharply against the brown pine-needle ground.

Where the forest hugged the upward sloping land, the trees were charred black, probably from a lightning storm over the summer.

He came to the first of the white and sugar pines that were scorched. The heart of the fire had burned the pines and hemlocks the worst, and the ground was still barren with patches of wild grass and buckbush just beginning to break through. The tree trunks were black with some of the trunks a little further north split in half or cracked and bending over. It looked like someone dumped black paint on the landscape. It was eerie walking under the tall pine-less black trunks, but he knew most of the pines, except for the badly damaged ones where the fire burned the longest, will be fine after some time. New bark will grow, and after the trees heal, scars will only be identifiable inside after a tree has been cut down. The land would heal from this.

He walked silently through the fire burned forest.

Samuel looked up as a dark hummingbird back flipped from the top of a soot-coated pine down onto a lower branch. It was beyond the burnt pines where he saw the wolf prints. It was a huge wolf, the footprint almost as wide as his own. He followed the prints north-northwest, parallel to the river, then east, before losing the track in the pine needles and finding the track again running towards the river in the gray soil past the Blue-Eyed Mary wildflower bushes that would bloom in May.

He felt like a wolf, a little old, a little tired, and just wanting to go a little further before he would rest.

***

When he looked up and to the right on the trail the next morning there was the American kestrel. It had to be the same one he had seen at the creek. If he had not looked up, he would have passed right under her. She was perched in a tree not more than 10 yards off, her talons gouged in a dead field mouse. The falcon kept her attention and talons on the mouse, tearing into the flesh with her hooked bill.

She yelled one single high-pitched call, before flying off the branch, the black patches across the wings and the tip of her narrow tail feathers, wings beating and then wings open.

The kestrel clutched the mouse close to her body for the least wind resistance. Even though it was a small mouse, it was a big catch for a kestrel that is roughly half the size of a red-shouldered hawk. She flew directly overhead, and the photographer of birds shifted so he could get a shot through the canopy. He stepped up on the downed pine snag, which gave him a clear shot. He waited so that the first photo was good. He had it. It would be a very good shot. With this lens and the medium shutter speed, along with the setting adjusted to compensate for the lower light and the smaller depth of field Samuel wanted, the kestrel's eyes would be in the sharpest focus in the photo. The rest of the falcon and its prey would be in focus also, except maybe the outer edge of the wings, which would be slightly blurred to capture the movement of flight. He hoped the top of the pines in the photographs blurred into a soft background to frame this spectacular shot.

Keeping his finger on the shutter release, he shot five more frames before the falcon was out of range, too far even for the 300 mm lens to capture. There was the rattlesnake, when he looked down, lying on the sun-lit side of the downed pine.

It lay stretched under the tree, its angled head resting on the fat part of its thick, scaled skin. It was at least four feet long. There was no rattle. No movement at all, until he started to back up, and the snake lunged and bit into his ankle, a clean bite through the pants and sock. He felt the fangs pierce flesh and the instant, sharp throbbing at the back of his neck, and then it was over. The snake slithered off, leaving a trail in the soil as it slithered.

***

Samuel sat down in the pine needles. He knew he should sit calmly for a little while to let the venom localize at the site before he tried to walk. It looked like both fangs broke flesh, one of them tearing into the vein that ran vertical at the base of his shinbone. At first there was a lot of blood, but it could have been the anticoagulants in the venom. The bite would hurt soon. He felt cold with the wind, and the back of his neck still throbbed, but his ankle around the bite was warm. If he'd worn looser-fitting pants, maybe the fangs would not have gotten through to flesh.

After twenty minutes, he began to walk back south along the trail. He remembered his cell phone stowed in his rucksack. There wasn't reception even back at the forest-service trailer, but he brought it with him out of habit. He turned it on. Maybe it would work here in the higher elevation. The keypad lit up, and the screen showed that it was 11:26 a.m. There were no bars. He hoped it might just be taking a few moments for the phone to pick up a signal. When the phone read 11:27 a.m., there was an X in the corner of the screen through the antenna.

He sat down and took a sip of water from the thermos. He looked at the viewfinder. The photo of the kestrel, for what it was worth, was a damn good one.

The Curlew would be migrating north now, just arriving here. Each bird would be thin and undernourished, worn from traveling seven thousand miles to this place, flying over six countries and three thousand miles of ocean, rhythmically moving their wing muscles, continuing on, aware only of the rhythm of their heart.

He flipped open his phone—the red X was still there. It was 11:55 a.m, but he felt like it was much later. When he tried to get up, his hand pushed down on a shard of thorn. He felt the thorn vaguely. It didn't distract him from the burning pain in his ankle. His legs felt as if they were moving a second behind his mind and he was about to sit down again when he decided he would have to cover some ground. He decided he would calculate a plan, mile by mile, and he would calmly execute it. He reached the previous night's camp, according to his plan, and stopped at the brook. He sat on the edge of the water and washed the bite with bar soap and some water, and filled the jug with some water that he would boil later.

He continued down the trail towards the open prairie.

When he sat down to rest again, he saw that his ankle was beginning to swell, and he felt it now, that severe pain deep where the fang marks were. It hurt worse when he tried getting back up, and he felt like he was going to vomit. But when he was moving he felt better, felt steady, nearly forgot about the pain, and he calculated mileages and directions in his head. He would keep to a plan. A plan, focus, goals with each step, and he would keep to his goals. He will have to keep to it, he thought.

You're breathing well, walking all right, everything is working according to plan, that's funny you know, you will keep to it, the plan, and your foot is not burning with every step. You can't feel the venom as if it is in your bones. Yes, keep telling yourself these things.

It was his damn fault, but it was one mistake, no, it was not his fault, nor the rattler's fault, it was something that happened in four seconds, four seconds that are history now.

You can hold off on writing the guidebook to dying in the woods. You're going to hike out of the woods, with or without a leg, but you've got a calculated plan, and it is no different than the hike in.

***

The small tin was in the bottom interior pack pocket. Inside the tin there were two items his wife had given him when she got ill, after the doctors found the cancer cells metastasizing. He held the smooth stone surface of the charm. It was a horse carved from Appalachian soapstone that her grandmother had made for her. She used to wear it until the eyelet broke, and she handed it to him years after it was handed to her. No, he would not accept it, he told her—he would not accept that her possessions would no longer be hers, he did not want it. But she wanted him to have it, to take it with him wherever he went. So he took it in his hand, holding tight the smooth stone.

He held the same stone tight, he felt its smoothness and its minute folds. It was the luxury he allowed himself, a moment to sit and remember, and soon he would get back to the calculations, the plan, the miles ahead. He did not take out the other item she had given him. He kept that in the tin for when he would need it.

When he stood up, it was harder to breathe, he had to focus on each breath, and he felt like he was going to throw up, until he began hiking, and he was able to focus on the movement. He was able to breathe then. For some reason, everything felt okay when he was moving ahead, ticking away the miles he had to go. He figured he was about halfway back to the trailer, which was then another three or four miles from the ranger station.

He stopped a mile, or two maybe, shy of where he camped that second night on the hike in. So he was about halfway, maybe even slightly more than halfway, he calculated. It was an hour before dark, and there was no point to going on. He would have to stop and try to sleep through some of the night, even if only three or four hours. When he was trying to set up the tent, he felt drunk, but when you're drunk, he thought, at least you feel like you have control. He couldn't put the tent poles in the top of the tent where they slid in. The nausea came back, and he leaned over thinking he would throw up. He lay the unfolded tent down flat, and put the sleeping bag over it, and laid down on it, tired, as tired as he had ever been. He pulled a fleece and shirts out of his pack and he lined the clothes behind his neck and he wrapped socks and another shirt around his neck and chin. He felt a littler warmer.

***

When he woke, in the cold night, half of his body was frigid numb, but from his waist down he felt his blood burning in his veins. He forced himself to eat a granola bar, to direct his attention away from the snake bite on his ankle, and after a few minutes he stood up, before he wouldn't be able to, and forced himself to hike a good two or three miles, slowly, trying not to think too much about the hike ahead still, and he sat down when he knew he couldn't walk any further. The sun was just coming up, golden and bright—warmer and warmer, his back was against his rucksack, his trusty chair, so comfortable, the rucksack was the best of chairs, a portable, comfortable chair.

Remembering now a morning long ago in the quiet sunny bungalow, his boy drinking milk and the cat, always wise and intuitive and loyal as a cat gets, came up and sat on the table. Remembering his son letting the cat drink out of the glass, tilting the glass so the cat could get his rough lion tongue to the milk. Remembering how he had watched and let his boy tilt the glass for the cat, the cat who would grow to love the boy and sleep in his room, and when the boy started going off to school, the cat old and very wise then, would sit by the window and wait for the boy to come home.

He would go on, but he needed more rest. He leaned back into his pack. He was not so far really, closer at least, but he can't go any further, not now. He can, he thought. No, he will soon enough though, before the noon hour. He felt a grin, as the words of the song drifted, so he caught it and sang along, sang about dogs and glasses of beer in the cowboy's dreams, sang it in his head, silently, because he didn't want to add noise to the environment other than his soft breathing.

He felt sleep overcoming him. He could sleep now, why not, he thought, and sleep finally came, or that state between sleep and wake when one is still aware of the time passing by. At one point he awoke from a dream as fragmented as ice splinters.

He woke, shivering, his head spinning and his leg numb, but it was all part of the dream—until the dog let out a bark and circled around the man laying down. The dog stopped and howled and looked at the man, and Samuel knew for sure it wasn't a dream. The dog whimpered and barked.

The he saw Thomas, tall, wide, bearded, a tree, part of this wild land.

Thomas half carried, half dragged him for a long distance to the truck. When Samuel awoke again, he was half covered with a thick blanket and leaning against the window in the backseat of the truck cab.

"I'm glad you didn't die on me."

Samuel looked over.

"It's a joke. Not a good one. You slept for most of the ride. The clinic isn't far from here."

The truck bounced through a sippy hole, the leaf springs creaking. The dog sat up in the front seat leaning against the door panel, steadying himself as the truck's suspension leveled.

"Shortcut," Thomas said. "They have a supply of antivenom. You sure it was the Western Rattler? Tan with dark brown and gray marks? A dark blotch along the sides of its head?"

"Yeah. That was it."

Outside the window, a falcon glided, a kestrel, beating its wings, soaring, flying in between the road and the power lines, as if the kestrel was racing the truck, until it shifted its wings, white against amber-blue sky, and veered across the road towards the pines.

Thomas asked how long ago it happened, the snake bite, and Samuel felt dizzy as he tried to think of time, "Yesterday morning," he said and remembered how he had tried to use his cell phone, "Eleven in the morning." The same falcon soared again beside the truck. It must have been the same one that he photographed, but now he was carrying a snake in his talons. The snake was four times the size of the falcon, drab tan and brown compared to the blue and orange of the kestrel that was almost like a faint flame. Samuel couldn't believe the kestrel had such a large prey in its talons, and then he saw that the talons were gripped into a rattlesnake that was somehow twisting upwards and beginning to wrap around the legs of the falcon. The rattlesnake arched and twisted and its cottonmouth was unhinged for a moment before it slammed closed, as the falcon became its prey. But the falcon kept flying somehow, for a few moments, before the bird began to drift from the sky. The snake swiveled in mid air as if to watch the helpless falcon with unblinking eyes.

CHAPTER FOURTEEN

June 26
Leaving Winter Beach, Florida

"This is it?" Karia said when she saw the car. "Is it American?"

"French. Peugeot."

"I like the color."

She stood motionless before the car door a metallic color halfway between green and blue. She glanced in at the white vinyl seats, as if she could see herself opening the door and sitting down. But she couldn't move. He stood with his hand on the chrome driver's door handle, waiting for her.

A woman in a blue dress and high heels clik clatt clik clatt rushed back to work from lunch. The woman's face was a long square like the other people who rushed back to work in the world. On the other side of the street, two kids skateboarded down the sidewalk, a cat scurrying out of the way. Karia stood there as if held in place by invisible cables.

"You okay?"

"Yeah, I think so. We should get going."

"Okay," he said and opening the door, he got in. His hand had the key in the ignition, and he waited for her.

In one clean step she got in, the cables snapping. She leaned back in the seat and shut the door. He started the car. It idled rough, and he let it run for a minute before putting it into drive and stepping down on the long gas pedal. He headed onto the narrow street that ran into 8th Avenue in one direction and in the other direction, their direction now, towards Atlantic, eventually the exit from town. A few drops of rain collected on the windshield. The sky is the same color as the car, she said.

The Peugeot was running smooth at a steady sixty five. She noticed how the car would rev high when he'd try to pass a slow-moving truck.

"So this is all new territory?" he asked.

"Yeah." She was looking out the window at the pine trees and swamp bordering I-95 that had replaced the billboards and construction barricades. The rain never came. Only those few early drops. The sun grew bolder and was now showing his face against the sky a brighter green hue.

"There's not much to see for a while," he said.

"How many miles is it to Idaho?"

The cars and big rigs were all in a hurry to pass through to somewhere else, and a silver SUV doing ninety rocked the small car like a yacht passing a rowboat in its wake. The dash made a low rattling noise, and Karia rubbed it gently.

"Idaho is a long way. We've got eight states to go," he said. "Nine, I forgot Kentucky."

The cars and trucks passed.

"Can you pull over? I feel..." she asked as they neared the first blue sign for the rest stop. He swung the car into the right lane before she finished the question. He let up on the gas, merging into the exit lane before the next sign. The car vibrated gently, a rebellion against the sudden decrease in acceleration. The Beatles sang about letting it be, whispering words of wisdom on the radio.

She got out at the rest area, mile marker 168, off I-95, and made it to the grass in front of the bathrooms when the cable clinked. Ryan stood by the car. She could tell he wasn't sure if he should give her space or help her. She looked over trying to tell him with her expression to give space, that she would be okay eventually. She bent over and threw up onto the grass. She braced for it to get worse, and it did before the anxiety attack was over. She called these moments storms, the moments when the cables snarled tight around her, when it became harder to breath the more she tried, when her legs would shake uncontrollably yet feel dead numb, when she would feel sick to her stomach, and the images around her all were a form of squares, circles, everything in geometry.

Maybe she shouldn't have stopped taking the Zoloft and Imipramine. Who cares if they had only made her feel numb to the world, she was finally getting used to it. To not seeing the things she once saw in rich colors. To her hands moving in slow motion. And to the rain she used to hear so vividly, a song of roof splashes and gutter drips, a perpetual, dull thud. She always felt like drifting asleep, even if she had just slept ten hours. If she stubbed her toe, she couldn't feel. She cut herself while dicing onions for soup she was cooking and sliced into her thumb. If it wasn't for the blood, she wouldn't have known she cut herself. *"That's the drugs working,"* Francis, the cognitive therapist had told her. *"There is a negative to it, they make one less—able to feel some sensations, and that's why so many people don't like them at first, but they are working. Just give it some time, and you'll see that it's better."*

No, no, no, she wants to start feeling again. She wants to feel the sting when she cuts herself while dicing onions, not just see the blood, feel that quick pain when she stubs her toe.

***

Just outside Savannah, Georgia

She had learned you breathe best after a near drowning. The air is the cleanest.

She felt the stillness of sleep coming and soon it would wash over her. The anxiety attack at the rest stop drained her worse than a ten-mile run. She watched his hands on the steering wheel.

"I remember smelling alcohol on his breath," she said. "But alcohol doesn't make someone do what he did."

Ryan kept one hand on the steering wheel.

"I pushed him. He fell over like a drunk, and I thought that would be the end of it. He stumbled to the kitchen, and I hoped he would pass out on the couch or drink himself into a stupor until my mom got home.

"I didn't know what to do. I tried to fight. He came in sometime in the night. It wasn't that late. I had just fallen asleep I think. He—he was determined to finish what he started.

"I think it was about two weeks later when my mom told me she was going to leave for Atlanta because he found a good job there. I knew right off I wouldn't go with them. Nothing on earth could make me go. I stayed and that's the only thing that saved me.

"The day they were packing everything up, I remember being so scared, my stomach in a big knot and I couldn't breathe. I was scared they wouldn't leave. That they might stay."

The interstate was a long straight line, and the sun was a triangle emptying out its energy. The sun angled down on everything. She turned to see him, one hand on the wheel, looking over at her, and then a row of cars and a big truck passed them, shaking the tiny car again, and he took his right hand and held hers like it was the worn metal of the steering wheel.

Another row of cars rushed past, shaking the Peugeot in its wake.

***

South of Bloomfield, Illinois

At the gas station, an old man in a cowboy hat and jeans and sleeves-rolled flannel pulled up, his Silverado's bumper two feet higher than the small coupe. Karia watched Ryan walking into the station to get a bottle of cold water and ask if there's a Walmart in town.

The man at the counter and the man who drove up in the Silverado were talking to Ryan, the older man pointing in a straight line through the air to designate where they would finally turn off for Highway 150. Ryan thanked the men and headed out with a bag of pistachio nuts and a water. He fueled up the car, and slid in.

She switched the dial until stopping on Garth Brooks singing about the white line getting longer, and he turned right toward Highway 150.

"All they've got is country. But I like his voice," she said as they left the station, and the old coupe headed south on the straight lines of cracked asphalt through just-tilled fields to each side.

A lone horse peeked out from a weather-worn red barn. The farm's fence, patched neatly in places with newer wood, ran along the highway until the small white sign:

Welcome To The Township of Bloomfield, Illinois.

He glanced over at her. Intuitive. He wasn't like William, the one she'd dated for a little while, if you can call it dating. He wasn't like any man she'd known.

"How do you feel?" he asked her.

"Okay."

"How many states did I sleep through?"

"Some of Georgia and all of Tennessee and Kentucky."

Two boys sat on the roof of a station wagon with a row of small baskets lining the wagon's tailgate. A hand-painted sign read

Farm Fresh Asparagus and Fava Beans For Sale.

It was a cool, damp morning, and everything was still covered with the evening's rain. The boys gave the peace sign as the old coupe hummed past.

***

The thick hunting fleece, green with Winchester written across the front, in his hands, he smiled. She took it and slid it on.

Even the size Small was a little too long in the sleeves. "It's comfy," she said.

"It will keep you warm as a bear. It's going to be cold there at night."

She stood in front of the mirror, throwing her head back, imitating a model at the end of the runway, the fleece her designer blouse.

"You need boots."

He found the only pair in her size, solid black hiking boots with thick treads underfoot. When they walked out, the car was waiting, low-slung steel stretching into the morning and surrounded by freshly-laid parking lot with neat white stripes. She sat on the front seat with the door open, pulled on the fleece, and changed out of her sneakers, putting on long socks and the boots, lacing them tight. The boots tight-fitting and warm, she felt sleepy and happy like she was still in bed. Not at all like she was in a Walmart parking lot. But that could have been because of the quiet stillness. Only a few cars and mini-vans were parked close to the store entrance. On the other end of the lot, a kid worked on his Bronco, the hood up while he stood on the bumper, his hat backwards, focused on the intricacies of the engine compartment, not on a tractor trailer parked on the edge of the lot.

Ryan was looking at the open map, measuring the miles with his thumb and index finger an inch apart. A lone crow walked in the pale sun. The bird stopped, bobbed up, stared briefly, and then walked to the grass.

"When I was four or five, there was this crow that would hang out outside my window," Ryan said. "He would be there every morning. I couldn't look out the window, but I could hear him. It might have been his *caw caw* scream outside my window, or how big he was. He seemed huge to me. I was just a kid, and I was so scared of that bird."

The crow—smaller than the cawing bird he described in his memory—picked up a scrap of sandwich crust in his beak.

"I remember my father told me this story about how the crow was once a beautiful rainbow bird." The bird walked off a few feet to protect his scrap.

"Like a wild parrot I guess, but even more beautiful with all these contrasting colors and a singing voice.

"But the story is that the crow flew too close to the sun one winter and his tail caught on fire. Before he got home, the bird's entire body was covered in soot, and the legend is that his tail was still on fire. The smoke and soot got into his throat, strangling his singing voice. He flew a long journey back home. When he got home, the crow gave the fire to the other animals, who had never seen fire before and were gathered in the snow. They lit wood to melt the snow and ice, freeing the small animals that were buried in snowdrifts, and keeping warm by the fire.

"That's why the crow is so black, but if you hold up a feather, you can see the trace of all these colors. His story was a lot longer. That's the part I remember."

The sun was breaking through the clouds, and Karia was looking at the faint rainbow of colors in the crow feathers. "You can see the rainbow," she said.

The crow remained, eating the parking-lot scraps, when they left. The country station played a steady twang on low, as they drove on through the greens of the flat farmland.

Leaning back in the seat, she wondered how he saw her. Her hair grew this long because she hadn't had it cut in a while. That morning she tied it in a ponytail. She felt how tired she looked. She remembered when he showed her the sketch he had made, her hair much shorter then, her eyes looking downward, the faint scar running from the edge of her eye across the top of her cheekbone like it was a chip in glass. Her skin like malleable marble. She never thought before about how she looked, never thought much about how others saw the scar.

"We're about halfway."

There was no one on the road except a few big rigs, Dodge and Ford pickups. "You think your father is doing okay?" she asked.

"He sounded better yesterday because they were letting him go. He said he wanted to drive."

"I thought the doctors told him he couldn't."

"They ordered him not to. I don't think it sank in, until they told him that he has to rest his leg the first week or two, and if he does something like driving across the country it could cause permanent nerve damage."

"I would be so scared."

"Yeah I know. It's weird," Ryan said. "I never worried about him. He's always going into the wilderness where there are no roads and cell phones don't work, and he never has a plan. Just exploring whatever ends up in front of him. But I never worried about him. It's what he does.

Maybe I just ended up thinking he would come through everything Okay. I never thought about how tough it would be on him.

"I think I've been too hard on him. I don't know. He's just been off in another world for so long. He didn't even go to my college graduation."

"Right after it happened?"

"Eight months after her funeral. He just stayed home. Everyone was there with their parents, all their friends, and I just looked out and saw no one."

"It's been tough for both of you."

"Yeah."

A light rain fell when they reached the hills of Missouri. He turned to her. "We can stop when we cross over into Nebraska."

***

Missouri-Nebraska state line

She felt his back curved against hers and heard a tractor-trailer passing outside. There was the sound of wind, another truck, and nothing. She began to drift to sleep in the occasional truck passing song of the Nebraska night, and woke in the morning holding onto a dream of light and water. There was an island, a circle of white-leafed trees and soft grass like she used to lay in as a child. Opening her eyes to Ryan brewing coffee in the small coffee maker, she was in between the hotel room and the dream. She liked the strong, dark smell of cheap coffee that filled the morning.

He started the car to let it warm up and took a sip of the coffee in the Styrofoam cup. She stood with her hands in the pockets of her fleece in the Missouri-Nebraska spring air, and she felt all right, looking out from the parking lot to the fuel stations and fast food restaurants and the sky beyond it all. She had never seen a white cloud formation as big as the one in the horizon between them and the Rocky Mountains.

He took another sip of coffee. "Two more states to go."

She leaned in, his lips varnished smooth bordered by grit sandpaper three-day stubble and his coffee breath, his lips like water and whiskey, and she was afraid to go back to half breaths and mornings cold to the touch. She looked up to the clouds.

***

Sidney, Nebraska

"Can you take over the helm for a little? Just a few miles," he asked when they passed the sign for Subway.

"I'll try. I think this is the straightest road in the country."

He pulled off the next exit, fueled up, and they split a steak sub. Karia slid into the driver's seat. Ryan looked at the map. She was jerky with the gas pedal, and over steered, but after a few miles, she was driving the old car in its rhythmic power range, adjusting to its quirks and letting the simple four-cylinder mill do its work. She passed a lumber truck and had it running just under seventy, the engine humming.

"We'll get to Salt Lake City just after ten," Ryan calculated.

She watched him looking out the window at the lemon pool of light splashed onto the asphalt every half-mile and the wave of hills in the distance. She could feel that he was watching her, and then he began to close his eyes. Sitting there in the capsule of steel and vinyl, a feeling of calm overcame her and she let out all the breath she had been holding in. She didn't want the car to stop. She wanted to keep going as far west as they could go.

Outside Salt Lake City, with the drone of the hotel's air conditioner, she whispered she was sorry. She would be able to let go, to feel him the way she felt him that night in the silence of her bathroom. But she needed time. Her therapist said this would happen. It's PTSD, he'd said—like the vets from Iraq? she had asked.

"I'm patient," Ryan said. "There's nothing to be sorry about. I'll wait ten years if I have to."

"Ten years?"

She kissed him on his cheek and on the lips.

"You won't have to."

She was just learning his lips, and his arms, his hands, and she would soon enough learn every other contour. There would be nights to learn when his hands strong and gentle would hold her.

***

National Forest, Solitudo County, Idaho

When they stopped at the ranger station, Karia listened to a thousand crickets competing in chorus from the forest that towered over the eastern edge of the narrow park road.

The tall ranger had to bend down at the car. So this was the man who had saved Ryan's father. His square chin had no expression, and his voice seemed to come from the forest behind him.

"You Ryan Leaton?" The tall ranger asked.

Ryan nodded.

"Thomas. I can take you guys over. You can park the car here."

A mile down the road, Thomas pulled the park-service truck off at the sign posted Park Service Access Only. The truck passed into a narrower space between two forests, two ruts of soil and patches of sunlight that cut through the dense mat of spruce and lodgepole and western pines. The trees higher and denser until the truck snarled up the steepest slope of the switchback trail onto the high ridge. The first thing she saw was the low juniper and sagebush growing in layers and tall grass everywhere. They came to the first of the white and sugar pines that were scarred black from the lightning fire. The tree trunks were black with some of the trunks split in half or cracked and bending over. He drove through the burned forest, and then to the north and west, they could see the river so clear the clouds swirled down on the surface; and rising up beyond the river the sloping twin peaks of a mountain.

"It's growing back. From the wildfire last summer," Thomas said, the first and only words he said until they got up to the trailer.

CHAPTER FIFTEEN

Old fire lookout trailer, Solitudo County, Wilson Sanford National Forest

Samuel saw the white box crawling north on the ridge long before he heard it.

When the government truck crept up the double-track, he was sitting back in the open doorway. Facing the sun, his one bare foot on the metal steps and the other wrapped in the cloth bandage. This had become his routine the past two days, early mornings facing the wind that smelled like clean, running river water and late afternoons facing the sun. Sitting on the metal steps, his face warm, he would almost forget he had no choice, forbidden from strenuous movements that still brought the sharp pain that would spread through his body, and the burning still in his ankle.

The sun of the late afternoon hung low in the west, now just above the mountains, bringing the day to the therapeutic close that Samuel needed more than the best medicine of the hospital. No amount of painkillers, sleep, whiskey, or anything else. That late afternoon sun was what he needed.

He couldn't put any pressure on his foot, so he sat there in the doorway and let the April afternoon sun warm his face. A pygmy rabbit munched bluegrass fifteen feet from the trailer this afternoon. The tiny rabbit was small enough to fit into the palm of his hands. Its ears picked up the distant drone of the truck's engine, and the rabbit dropped its small blade of grass and leapt off into the sagebush.

The truck crawled along the Jeep trail, and when the truck stopped and they came walking up, Thomas and his boy came up first, and he saw how long his son's hair had grown. His son was looking around, and he was carrying two big packs. Samuel wanted to walk down to them, but he had to wait there on the steps. The girl was behind them. She was skinny and wore a fleece too big for her. There was something about her. She was walking with shy, graceful steps through the setting sun's light.

"Hey, Dad."

"Hey, Ry." Samuel nodded to Thomas. "You must be Karia." He put out his hand.

"Does it hurt, Dad?"

"Not so bad."

Thomas helped Ryan carry the packs inside. He looked in the small fridge.

"When are you leaving?" Thomas asked Samuel.

"Morning after tomorrow I think."

"You don't have much food here."

"There are a few things in the cabinet."

Thomas looked in the cabinet. There was half a bag of rice, two cans of red beans, and a dust-covered tin of spam and a box of noodles that looked like someone had left a long time ago.

***

In the morning, Karia heard the crunching of tires on the trail that led to the trailer home when Thomas's white truck pulled up. Through the window, she saw Thomas walk up with Japhy behind him. He stood unhurried, and it seemed like he was smiling, or trying to smile, when she and Ryan stepped outside.

The dog came up to her slowly and hesitant, and she held out her hand. The dog dabbed his cold nose to her palm, one blue eye and one brown looking up at her. The shepherd husky turned and then walked back towards the truck.

"He likes you," Thomas said.

"Really?"

"You'd know if he didn't."

The dog sat down by the truck and watched them

"I've got to check a few of the traps," Thomas said. "I can show you some of the park, and then we can head into town. You can pick up some fresh groceries at Adamson's."

***

The forest service Dodge waited. Everything besides the new tires tucked under the fenders was dirty and worn. Dings, dents, and scratches decorated the bumper and hood. Thomas opened the back cab door, and Japhy looked confused.

"Gotta ride in the back. Up, up." The shepherd-husky jumped up. "Good boy."

Karia hopped up in the back, and the dog sniffed her jeans. The floorboard carpets no longer gray, stained with the dark remnants of spilled coffee and dirt. The interior smelled like wet dog. Ryan sat up front and slid the front seat forward.

A breeze came through as Thomas turned up the narrow Jeep trail. The truck slugged through the rutted, sandy soil. He stopped and put the truck in four-wheel-drive-low. He kept the wheels straight and his boot on the gas steady so the truck's tires gripped and didn't spin. The trail turned in a half-S at the top and after the turn, it went straight ahead as far as Karia could see. Thomas let the truck motor up the two-rutted trail. The dog curled up beside her. His fur was coarse and peppered with white strands. It was soft under the coarse collar coat of fur. It was soft like the fleece she wore.

Thomas got out and unlocked the fence by the sign:

Forest Service Access Only

And they passed another small tin sign posted to a pine:

Entering Conservation Area
No Hunting.

The dog looked out in anticipation, his nose out the window. As soon as the Dodge stopped, his tail was wagging. Thomas put the truck in park and grabbed his hat off the dash.

"Mind a hike?" he asked, and at the word *hike* the dog's ears pointed up. "It's a little ways."

"Let's do it," Ryan said.

They walked a good while through the tall thin pines into a big field that looked down over the river, until the trail took them through another dense grove of tall pines, these almost twice as wide and twice as tall. The top branches of the trees swayed with the wind. The dog went ahead of them, and would stop, tilt his head and wait until he heard them catch up before trotting ahead. The trail now went up, through glacial deposited rocks and under one huge pine, a Ponderosa, Thomas told them. It was a big, old tree with deep wrinkles in the bark and long, twisting branches.

There was no sound except the wind through the trees.

When she looked up they were moving through the edge of the darker forest. It was another country—open and gray under the largest trees she had ever seen—and cold in the sudden shade.

"How far are we from the nearest road?"

It was a silly question. She knew there were no paved roads for a long ways. But the silence had overwhelmed her, and she needed to say something to test if sound existed.

The trees blocked the wind but they could hear it smacking the top of the branches, which continued to bend away from the westerly wind, snapping back when it softened. The dog trotted ahead of them, stopping every so often until he heard footsteps catch up. The dog and the tall ranger hiked up the steep trail, the dog ahead of the man, and where the sun came down, the dog stopped on a boulder, smelling the wind, paws at the edge of the big rock, and Thomas not far behind, slowing his stride where the land leveled out. Ryan and Karia were maybe fifty yards or so behind. It was as if the man and his dog so familiar to this land were silent tour guides, stopping there, above the steep drop into another valley of ferns. A deer with her twin does munched on breakfast.

The hulk of the mountains that looked like a sleeping giant rose up along the horizon.

From there the trail switched back into the tall pines. Japhy ran on ahead into the pines where a moment later he started barking. Loud, ferocious barking. Thomas ran after him, sensing danger. After a few hurried strides, he could see three men. The dog must have smelled them well before the humans knew they were anywhere near.

Thomas slowed his approach as Japhy growled low, with the fur on the back of his neck standing up. He growled from his chest—a warning. Whatever he was smelling, he didn't like it. From their appearance, Thomas could imagine sweat, tobacco, and perhaps aggression too. To the dog, the odor of aggression riding the wind would have been unmistakable, just as the scent of fear was. Both unmistakable, but one so totally different from the other.

Thomas was right about trouble. He heard the man in front yell, "Where the hell did that dog come from?"

"Hell if I know," said the second man.

The man in front, the one who had first spoken, seemed to be the leader. He was stout with tattoos covering his forearms. Thomas was close enough now to pick up the smell of chewing tobacco and body odor. The man lifted his rifle. "I know where he's 'bout to go," he said, showing his stained teeth, as he steadied the weapon. Overpowering every other scent, the man's odor of aggression must have come straight at the dog, but Japhy would not be intimidated by the threat standing there, aiming his gun. The dog bared his teeth and growled, a low menacing growl, a warning.

"HEY! Down! Down boy," Thomas yelled in a tone the dog had only heard a time or two before. The dog listened, and stopped.

"Stay—stay," Thomas called to his dog. He approached carefully into the clearing keeping his gaze on the man with the rifle steadied on Japhy.

"Yeah, stay there dog," the leader said.

"He's staying. Lower your rifle."

Japhy stood still, growling at the men. Growling like he would charge at them any moment.

"He don't look like he's staying to me," the leader with the rifle said.

Damn you, just lower your rifle, Thomas thought. Damn you, damn you. The dog will stay if you'll lower your rifle.

"Stay boy. Easy," Thomas said, then he said to the stout man, "He ain't going nowhere. Lower the rifle." Thomas wondered where Ryan and Karia were, if they could see from where they were.

The man didn't lower the rifle. Thomas took a few steps closer to the dog. He didn't have his sidearm. It was back in the truck, under the seat. He watched the one who aimed the gun. Thomas saw a scorpion etched among the tattoo-covered forearms extending below a rolled-up flannel. The man was thirty or so, a man of medium height, with a close-cut, military-style haircut.

The next man in line also held a rifle, but kept if across his chest. He had long hair pulled back and a fu Manchu. The tattooed man had what looked like a .338 Winchester Magnum, and fu Manchu was also holding a .338, that one a semi-auto with scope and all-black stock. The third man, with the biggest gut of all three, stood behind the other two, and he appeared unarmed.

The third man called to the man with the rifle and pointed, but the stout man kept the rifle aimed at the dog growling from his chest.

Thomas should have his pistol. That he knew. He was a law-commissioned ranger, trained as an officer, which meant he was the law here. He could apprehend anyone suspected of violating federal law, and he carried all the things sheriff's deputies do. But he wasn't the same as a sheriff's deputy. That's for sure. He should have his gun, but he was no sheriff's deputy. *Damn you, you want to test what I am.*

Karia and Ryan came into the clearing, and Karia grabbed Japhy by the collar. That was brave, but she'd put herself in the line of fire. Thomas didn't want that.

Now he had to add the kids to the equation. He went from wishing he had his gun to thinking a firearm wouldn't be any good in this situation with these men.

The tattooed man kept the rifle pointed. It wasn't exactly clear where—at the dog still growling or the girl now holding the dog.

Japhy tried to shake free. The dog wanted to get at the man with the rifle now. But she held tight, until it looked like she couldn't hold onto him. That's when Thomas rushed up and got a hold of the collar, as he grabbed a tight grip on it he pulled a few strands of thick fur from the dog's neck. Thomas yanked the dog back, hooked the leash on and anchored it around a tree. "Stay here," he said.

Stout man and fu Manchu were huddled, holding their rifles like umbrellas, and the third guy, standing behind the others, seemed to be saying by the look on his face, "What the fuck are you two doing?" Even so, he didn't have any sway over the other two. It was clear who the leader was.

"What's your name," Thomas asked the tattooed one.

"Jim Timmons. That damn dog—"

"You know there's no hunting here?"

Thomas was studying his face, fixing in his mind exactly what the man looked like. It was a face that wouldn't be hard to remember.

"You know that?"

"Naw, we didn't know it," the tattooed one finally said, backing down.

Japhy was barking, pulling at the leash so hard that bark snapped from the tree.

"You got your ids?"

Thomas noticed the expensive, clean boots the man had, the leatherman and Nextel on his belt, and expensive-looking watch. None of them wore camo hunting overalls or worn boots—the attire of the backcountry hunter. And no one was saying Sir to him. Fu Manchu stood next to a black case, some kind of binoculars maybe.

"You're standing in the middle of a conservation area. You work at the drill? You work for Centur?"

"Why's that matter," the tattooed man said with a cringe of his lips. Thomas thought that one was a real son of a bitch. He studied his face.

"None of us work for Centur," said fu Manchu.

"There is no hunting here," Thomas said, "It's well marked."

"Yes sir," said the quiet one speaking to Thomas for the first time.

"Where's your truck?"

Fu Manchu pointed back west towards the other of two Jeep trails that led into these woods.

Thomas knew he'd done enough already with the kids there. And he had to get Japhy out of there too. Something was funny about those boys, something that he didn't want to discover when it was two rifles against none. On the way out he passed their Expedition. It was on tall tires, 38s or 40s. Black with dark tinted windows, blacked-out headlights, a 12,000-pound winch on the bull bar, and a row of KC lights.

***

Karia had studied the man's face too, and she remembered the man's teeth and the violence webbed into his face.

She'd seen men like him before. She knew what they could do. There is a long list of things they can do. They can burn scars into your flesh and make it hard to sleep at night while they're free to walk away. She tried to shut out the hatred she had for all the men with those lines in their faces. She tried to shut out her own violence, so she turned to the dog and caressed him gently where the fur was soft under his collar. The dog was curled up on the blanket Thomas had folded over the seat. The dog eye's were shut, and he was breathing lightly, relieved that the threat was gone. She breathed lightly too. The truck bounced along and the engine revved when it climbed higher. The dog awoke and looked up for a moment before he put his head down, resting his muzzle against the girl. The truck kept bouncing along, and the dog went back to sleeping like a pup.

CHAPTER SIXTEEN

Nebraska/Missouri line

Just as Ryan and Karia came in the door, holding the coffees and a bag from the diner next door, the rain finally came, and the thunder rumbled through the walls.

Ryan put the coffee down on the hotel table. "You were right, Dad. Here's yours."

"Hopefully it clears soon," his father said.

"Are you hungry?" Ryan asked.

"Just coffee would be good."

"We got some muffins," Karia said.

"Thanks." His leg was up on the small sofa, his ankle rested on one of the pillows.

"It's good that we're not on the road," his son said. Through the blinds they could see all light drained from the skies. The rain splashed onto the parking lot outside the door, and the thunder was crashing as if it was just outside the walls.

"You want the banana nut?" he asked.

"Yeah."

Karia went into the bathroom, and Ryan went to pack up a few things in his bag. His father gazed out at the rain through the blinds.

Ryan sat on the chair opposite the couch.

"You think it will let up soon."

"Hopefully."

"How does it feel?" his son asked.

"Okay."

"You can move it?"

"More than yesterday."

"Thomas said you're planning on going back."

"To Idaho?"

"Yeah."

"I'm going to try," Samuel said.

"For the Stilted Curlew?"

"Yeah, I'm going to try. What?"

"No, I was thinking, what if you don't, will anyone else try, to find the Curlew, I mean?"

"I don't think so."

"No one cares?"

"No one has any hope anymore."

The rain came down on the roof, and his son got up and went over to the window.

He looked out through the half-open blinds. "What do you think Mom would want you to do?"

The doubt that Samuel had questioned earlier stung in the base of his brain. Yet he knew she would understand when he went back. She would have known he had to, that he couldn't give up, not yet. She knew what kind of man he was.

"I think she would tell me to go back."

BOOK II

CHAPTER SEVENTEEN

Winter Beach

Scaly flesh coiled tight, its wide head poised, and the eyes, beady, unblinking, staring. Samuel turned, a reflex, but he knew he didn't have time to step away. And he knew the snake would fix the unblinking eyes at him until it lunged out— uncoiling into a strike. It was within striking distance of its target. It stared. Empty beady eyes with the darkness of its thin vertical pupil, the snake had already decided what it had to do. That's why there was no rattle. The eyes reflected all light and color but no emotion from within the animal.

When he woke, there was the silence of the house's interior, and then the light and distant sounds of a car passing somewhere, and the eyes were not gone. The numbness of the painkillers had worn off, and there was the pulsating sting, and there would be no sleep. The darkness of those eyes was engrained in the darkness of night.

Samuel sometimes had a hard time sleeping that first night when he came back from a trip. He would think of the photographs, anxious to see them on the computer screen, to discover which ones surprised him, the ones that would show the beautiful nuances of flight. But he had fallen fast asleep that night soon after he went down on the bed, and he slept for maybe an hour or two before, from the deepest tiredness, the beady black eyes looked in.

When he woke, he went down to the painkillers on the counter, and then to his study, shifting aside the papers and books that had grown over his desk like a vine spreading.

He clicked on the lamp and lowered it so it shined on the Nikon. He sat down at the desk, four fifteen in the morning, and began to take apart the camera, removing the lens from the camera box to examine the chip on the glass and to clean the sensor. The chip was a quarter-inch deep in the outer lens glass, but the elements inside the lens looked okay, and the focusing ring was working. Nikon had stopped making this lens model, and the new model included vibration control, auto functions, and was built using more plastic than ever. The new lens was lighter, yet less durable. But the major drawback is the loss of user flexibility that often comes with more computerized technology incorporated into the most modern high-tech lenses. And now they are building these new mirrorless cameras that are half the size and weight of the digital camera boxes. They say these new cameras will replace the older Nikons and Canons, that until something else comes along that is as close to holding nothing in your hand as possible.

He wasn't against all of the new photography technology. Some of it allowed photographers to capture images that would have been impossible with older equipment. But at some point, the technology just puts another level of separation between the photographer and their subject. His old broken lens was the right combination of technology and basic internal geometry that worked well. It was simple to use, while allowing the photographer in the field to quickly choose the settings that mattered. He would get it repaired.

The camera box was in good shape besides a few new scratches on the bottom. But it was that lens he really cared about. He hoped the shop could repair it.

The lenses were different over the past fifteen years, since he mailed in his first set of photos to *Birding World*, the beautiful shots of an adult roseate spoonbill landing down at dusk. That spoonbill came out of nowhere as he was hiking back to the truck. He hoped the bird would land down, as he fumbled to get the camera out of his pack—he learned that afternoon to always keep the camera ready—and focused on the spoonbill flying thirty yards off. The Smithsonian lists the spoonbill as one of the most striking birds found in North America. An image of the roseate spoonbill was also etched into the worn cover of *Southeastern Birds* guidebook that he kept in his pack.

It did land, and he focused the lens. The spoonbill was even more beautiful as it spread its huge roseate-hue wings to gain balance atop a tree. The pink plumage and red shoulders came in clear focus through the ancient, but gently-used AI Nikkor purchased at a yard sale. With a sturdy rubber manual focus ring and metal outside components, that old AI was one of the most mechanically sound lens Samuel ever owned. It fell over a kayak into the Florida marsh, twice, dropped out of the truck, got wedged between a rock and a cliff in Virginia, and it kept working. When Samuel bought his first brand-new camera two years later he had to get a new lens because the older one wouldn't fit the coupling on the new camera.

It was this AF-d lens, his first good lens, with a faster focus speed and six elements inside the lens, that he had when he was out on the other side of the Glades where the western edge of land meets the Gulf that early morning he photographed that Bachman's warbler, the rarest songbird in North America. And it was that same lens that captured the peregrine falcon diving down on its prey like a bullet through the Wisconsin sky.

Lorine got him the newer Nikon E lens one Christmas. She gave it to him two weeks before Christmas, put the box there on the kitchen table for him to discover in the morning, because he was heading out on a trip in a few days. That was the same lens that captured the American kestrel in Solitudo County, Idaho. Combining the best of modern design inside the lens and using durable metal components outside, the lens he now examined was better than anything they make today.

***

She had slept in that morning—as she had grown accustomed to sleeping in until eight on Saturdays—and he woke early every day. Those mornings he woke first, she would stir a little before tucking herself into the comforter like a mallard tucked in close to her feathers on a cool morning. She would fall sound asleep again after he got up. He always said she could sleep through a bulldozer tearing the house down.

He woke and went to the kitchen to start the coffee and breakfast as he usually did when he was home, and he saw the box on the table. He just looked at it, and when he ran back to the bedroom, she was tucked under the thick comforter, but he could see she was half awake.

"Did you go to the kitchen?" she asked, and she smiled when she looked up and saw his expression brighten.

***

Solitudo County

The waitress came by, and they ordered a coffee. Oscar had worked for Centur Corp. for exactly fourteen months before he had stopped going to work that cold November day two years

127

earlier—he'd take his chances trying to make it on unemployment and odd jobs rather than clean dead fish from the river's shore. And now he wanted to meet with Thomas.

That's because he remembered something his pap had said about Thomas. "He's the only one of 'em you can trust," Oscar's pap said. "The rest are all Scottson's trolls, or worse in the damn pocket of Centur Corp." When Thomas first started working for the park service, Oscar's old man was his boss. From time to time, the two would go fishing, up until Oscar's father retired. A few years before, Thomas and Oscar's uncle, along with Oscar, had gone on a trip fishing Snake River.

Oscar suggested the truck stop out on Route 7. Outside the sign read:

Try Our BBQ Ribs. Nothing Else Like It.

But they weren't here for barbeque.

"That far north? Damn. That can't be," Thomas said.

Oscar looked out the window. Thomas wasn't sure at what, but from here you can see the pines on the southern edge of the forest.

"I just wanted to tell someone," Oscar said, "but hell it seems like it's a done deal. If there is anything that can be done—I mean, shit they'll put a thousand drills in this land if they can. My pap told me how they bought up half the county back when the logging companies first came in, without anyone knowing that it was for logging. My uncle sold four hundred acres of old growth south of his ranch that he thought was going to be used as hunting land."

The waitress filled their coffees and then made her way to the only other occupied tables. At one a man sat with his wife and a small girl, at the other table in the corner, a trucker watched CMT videos on a small TV and ate his breakfast.

"How do they even imagine they'd get the rigs up there to build a pipeline?" Thomas asked.

"A road."

"They can't build a damn road."

"They think they can," Oscar said. "I think that's really what they want from Canson. They'll build an access road on his property and a bridge over Wolf River, then up to the lake."

"From Wolf River it's an elevation grade of two miles up every mile out."

"They're going to try like hell, Thomas. They've got enough gas under that lake floor to try to move the mountain."

"I ran into a few of the Centur Corp. boys a couple of weeks ago," Thomas said. "They gave me and Japhy a surprise. Said they were out hunting. Had some high-powered rifles to prove it. I wasn't sure, but I'd seen one of those boys at the test drill."

"Where were they?"

"North of Highline Ridge, just northeast of Shadow Pass."

"Shit. Driving a jacked-up Expedition?"

"Yeah. You think they were surveying for a road—up that far north?"

"Them boys weren't hunting," Oscar said. "Probably surveying. That's why you saw them that far north. They're fixing to build a road right through there."

CHAPTER EIGHTEEN

A week later
Winter Beach, Florida

The regulars are those who lose time sitting in their corner, the last ones filling their mugs again long after the bankers or the realtors leave their empty plates and mugs behind. They are fixtures and consistencies like the old espresso maker that often inspires her uncle to say "they don't make 'em the way they used to" or the worn keys on the register. She liked it most when the afternoon crowd thinned. The two old men drinking their espresso under the dim light, a chessboard on the table between them at their usual table. Joel at the counter in his Red Sox cap talking baseball with the mailman stopping in for his scone before he heads home. And Karia's uncle moving in quiet efficiency all over the place, nervous about the meeting with the building inspector.

In the corner behind the two old men, in coffee-and-paint-stained jeans and a thin flannel, before his sketchpad open, his hands rummaging across the paper, she could see he was using blue charcoal. She could see his hands exploring, dredging, excavating, searching, circling, sensing, catching, sifting. He was losing the remainder of the day, looking at the sketchpad and glancing up at the two old men lost in their chess match.

The light snuck around the other buildings into the windows twice a day, early in the morning and later in the day, and the setting sun was shining through the glass. Her uncle closed the blinds, but that couldn't keep the light out. She thought about taking chances, only one or so a day. It was a weird thought, but she tried not to analyze it.

She looked over at Ryan, the focus of her rebellion that night.

She wiped down the espresso machine, and she watched him in the neat small space he built on the café table.

"Karia," her uncle called.

"Karia."

"Yeah."

"When Bill gets here can you make him a latte. I think that's what he drinks. Well, I'll make sure. But whatever it is he wants, I want you to make it."

"Okay."

With the blue charcoal, making short angled marks in the paper, Ryan began drawing the colors underneath.

***

In the cool night, Karia swung her feet over the side of the platform, and looked down between her toes before she jumped off. "The sand is cold," she said.

She stepped over the thin shadows and walked to the big tic-tac-toe board. She sat down in the sand of the quiet, empty, nighttime playground, the coarse sand cold under her feet.

"When I was little, I would ride my bike up and down the street," she said. "This makes me think of those days. A long time ago."

Ryan stood under the monkey bars.

"I remember my mom would always be watching me. I was nine or ten and you couldn't get me off that bike. I would think she forgot about me, and when I rode back by she would be there, standing in the doorway keeping watch over me," she said.

"That was when it was just me and her. That was before she changed. Before she thought she needed someone else."

"Is that when she met your stepfather?" he asked.

"There were some before him. Each one was worse than the asshole before. It was as if they all had to take control of everything because they saw how close we were. And she let them. She let each one break her apart a little more, and break us apart. I think about the way she was before, and I want to forgive her. I try to just remember those days and forget everything else she did. I've tried. I try to think about what she would have been like if she didn't change like that— I'll always have this scar, and I won't be able to forgive her."

He sat down next to her in front of the tic-tac-toe board.

"I'll always have it." She took his hand. "Feel it? Here."

When she took her hand away he kept his fingers there.

"You don't mind it."

"No," he said.

She pushed her toes into the sand.

"How much do you think about your mom?"

"She would laugh if she knew how much," he said. "She'd say, 'Ry, you're a little crazy.'"

"You're not crazy."

***

Solitudo County

When he came into the Ranger Station, Thomas saw the previous day's newspaper. The story was on the front page below the fold.

Centur Corp. led by new Gas CEO Seeks "200 drills" in Solitudo

Staff Report

The Independent-Tribune

Solitudo County--Yesterday at a public forum, Centur Corporation representatives talked about more jobs and economic impact from increased shale gas drilling, and how the company would respond quickly to any reports of possible water contamination.

Centur's new CEO of Natural Gas Operations, Edward Masey III, spoke publicly for the first time in his new position with the energy company. The meeting at the county administration's auxiliary building was the first of several public meetings required before the company begins the next phase of a gas-drilling process called hydraulic fracturing—also known as hydrofracking—on lands within Wilson Sanford National Forest.

Survey work and exploratory gas drilling is already underway in the national forest.

"These are big projects that are really important," Masey said, "and it means jobs and it means work." A recent study by the University of Idaho, Masey pointed out, calculates that the ramped-up natural-gas production would mean up to 65,000 jobs, averaged over a fifty-year period.

Centur Corporation is moving ahead with plans for a total of "up to two hundred natural-gas drill sites throughout Solitudo County" in the next two years, Masey said. The corporation lobbied for legislative changes championed by Governor Scottson that allowed companies to begin drilling on federally-preserved land in the northern half of the county. Exploratory drill permits on national-forest land were first issued in March, 2009, and additional drilling work will take place throughout the rest of this year.

The expanded drilling throughout Solitudo County will become "higher profile" in the national debate as the number of drill sites triples in the county and Centur Corp. drills its second site in Wilson Sanford National Forest this spring. Additional hydrofracking is also expected in adjacent conservation areas.

Opponents say the environmental risks are too high to allow such drilling to continue on federally-protected land. These lands are classified as critical habitat for threatened species such as Caribou and Wolverines.

Resident Tim Abott was one of thirteen residents to speak at the meeting: "God gave us this place for a reason, and we have to protect it."

Several residents and representatives from the local business and construction industry also spoke in support of the drilling, including a group that stood outside with signs, some of which read "*Get the Gas. Save our Economy.*"

Masey, Centur Corp's new CEO resigned from his position as Southeast Director at Conoco-Phillips last month so he could take over as the second-highest paid executive at Centur.

Houston, Texas-based Centur Corporation is currently the seventh-largest gas exploration company in the U.S., and the company was awarded a bid to drill on upwards of ten thousand acres throughout northern Solitudo County. The Company is first in line for additional bids to drill on federally-protected lands. Industry experts expect exponential growth for the company now that legislators approved changes allowing gas drilling and production on federal lands. Scottson, backed by the support of a growing corps of Republican politicians, is pushing for the increase to happen "today."

"Anyone who really cares about providing jobs in Idaho, would support natural gas production anywhere possible in our state," Scottson said.

***

The lean, searching wolf stood on the riverbank. The wolf, long-legged, white-faced, looking into the water, sniffing the rocks. The wolf unaware of the two men above—their clumsy footsteps down the trail still too distant to hear. The wolf unaware of the machines and the poison that would kill more fish. Old eyed, looking out, the wolf now heard the men approaching, and was gone, disappearing back into the pines.

By the river, it was easy for the two men to work under the full moon shining down like a spotlight installed for the constructions of men.

They placed thirteen dead fish into a black trash bag. With his Maglite in one hand, one of the men bent down to pick up the thin, whitish-transparent fins broken from the fish.

When they finished, four a.m., there was no trace of the asphyxiated, bloated fish that slowly sucked in the carbon seeping into the water a half-mile from the drill.

CHAPTER NINETEEN

Idaho Fish and Wildlife has tracked forty-three wolverines over the past decade, most of them in the mountain backcountry in the northern half of the state. This is the story of W-43.

Wilson Sanford National Forest

From up on the ridge Thomas could hear the pain in her growl of a cry. The cry cut through the air, coming from the river about a mile away. He gathered what he could from the forest service truck—the pair of gloves, a bundle of blankets, the discarded box in the bed of the truck, and a fishing net—as if any of it would help him capture the wounded animal.

Her eyes glowed dim and weakly. She was dehydrated, probably left there trapped to rusted steel for a week or longer, but she was not weak nor desperate enough to let a human touch her. She wouldn't let anyone get near her, not without a vicious fight. She was an adult female, and Thomas was pretty sure she had a den somewhere between the river and the ridge.

Thomas had never seen a wild wolverine up that close, and this wasn't how he wanted to. His second winter in the forest he saw an adult and her kit trekking down the steep side of Shadow

Pass. Through the binoculars he watched the mom climbing down into the pass, with the kit following, his paws like snowshoes too, but his stride smaller, hesitating where the mom climbed over the rocks. The mom climbed down without looking back, and the kit stumbled to navigate the rocks. After the kit crossed the biggest rocks, he bounded down to catch up, as fast as he could run. The two small figures were barely visible through the binoculars and then gone.

The wounded animal growled and hissed at Thomas and lunged forward when he took another step. It was an absurd effort. He moved like a man, calculating and slowly, while she moved quickly and with all of the life she had left to keep him away. She ripped off one of the gloves that were open and lose fitting for landscaping work or stacking cords of wood, scraping her claws into his hand. She stood back victoriously, showing her teeth as a warning. Thomas turned to leave, facing the pines that grew above the river, and he heard the animal moving. He stopped and stood there at the ten-step distance, and she laid down just like a dog resting, with her front legs bleeding from where she had tried to gnaw through the steel teeth of the trap. She stared at him. The wolverine listened to his movement, and the pain burned through to the bone.

He knew they did this. The Centur Corp. men surveying for that pipeline, or another drill. They just didn't get a chance to finish the job yet. So his gut was right, that tattooed one wasn't carrying around that big .338 Winchester to make up for his looks.

The bleeding was getting worse where she chewed through the flesh, and it made him sick to look at it. That tattooed one was one of the zealous men who doesn't think twice about what they're trying to do, Thomas thought. The third one, the tall guy, he was quiet, and it looked like he didn't want anything to do with the two. Maybe he would quit the way Oscar had? There was something about those two other boys though.

"All right," he said, catching his breath, turning his attention back to the Wolverine. "You hate me. I get that."

He knew this was not how you should do this.

"I'm just going to put this old blanket on you," he said, "and then I'm going to grab you with these hands. You might not like it. But you don't have no choice. I'm not leaving here without you. All right?"

He thought the wounded animal was maybe listening. Well, she was paying attention as he stood there talking to the cold air. Hunched low, her leg twisted in the trap, her dirty fur caked in mud, the wounded animal started up at him. She closed and opened her eyes. The fight had drained what little energy she had left, but that didn't mean she wouldn't fight again.

Tift once told Thomas how researchers realized the Wolverines could smell the trace of humans left behind on the traps for weeks. Despite their strength and mythological aggression towards humans, they are one of the shyest mammals. Avoiding human contact at all costs, they need wide, open, wild territories. They're solitary roamers, but an adult female will stay near her den and protect her territory. She'll stay, and she'll do what she has to do.

They must have wiped down the traps with bleach before they put the bait in it. Must have wiped their scent right off the sharp steel.

"Don't be too rough on me," he said to the wounded animal looking at him.

He eased up to her like he was just walking up to a wounded dog. Dropping the blanket, he grabbed the bundle. He clutched his arms around the animal clawing and punching at the old wool wrapped around her. "No, this ain't how you do this," he said aloud to himself and the wounded animal, and he hoped the blanket and the flannel against his forearms would keep the claws from digging in.

***

Just before the sippy hole, he put it down in four low, and the truck barely made it across that deep mud that would be frozen in a few weeks, the box sliding on the seat as the animal tried its darndest to rip the cardboard in half. He held one arm down on top of the box until they were out on the asphalt entry road. The seat was covered in blood.

When the all-terrain tires hit the concrete curb stop, he shut it down, stepped out and carried in the bloody box wrapped in another flannel blanket. He carried it gently as the injured wolverine inside kept on scratching and trying to tear through. The vet met him at the door and took the box. With his foot, the vet pushed open the door to the back area of the wildlife animal hospital, and she was gone.

Back out in the cold rain, he shut the truck door and realized how much blood had spilled on the seat and the carpet, a streak of deep crimson from when the truck sank in the sippy hole and he had thought the box was going to rip in half.

It was getting dark, and he felt anger and something else that felt like loneliness maybe. It would get colder soon. It's the windy and wet days that make it bitter cold when that wind comes down from the mountains in November. But even in early October, the wind made him close up his flannel. He buttoned it up and stood outside for a moment. Back inside, he lowered into one of the chairs upholstered the same color as that pale gray that soaked through the window. He thought of the things he'd have to do the next day. He'd call Tift. She would want to come to the clinic. She would want to check around where the trap was, too. She would check for boot prints, anything left behind, a discarded cigarette or used hand warmer, any sign of whoever did this. She would want to send back what she could to the forensics lab. He would let Williams know too. Although he knew for sure who had set the trap that could have been out for weeks, it wouldn't be easy to prove it was the Centur Corp. men.

And he knew now what his feeling was. It was something like loneliness because no one could help you. It was the feeling of intense, gnawing hatred that he hadn't felt since he was a young man, a feeling that comes straight at you before you know it has arrived. It was a feeling that he had worked very hard to leave behind, and after he moved West he had started to forget the feeling that was planted in time and another geography.

He sat in the pale gray seat as they amputated the animal's front leg.

Tiredness took over as he drove home, letting the truck drift along at thirty on the narrow roads. The cold rain let up but the horses kept their noses inside Carter's red barn. It had been raining off-and-on for the past three days. When he pulled up to his place, Japhy greeted him at the door. Thomas petted the dog on the side, the dog leaning into him, thumping his tail against Thomas' leg and sniffing where some of the blood had dried.

***

Eighteen miles west of Winter Beach, Florida

Out in the early morning sunshine they walked down Albatross Road to Kingbird Lane to Ibis Court, passing two dozen homes that were evenly spaced out in the suburban neighborhood with streets named for birds before homes gave way to the strawberry and tomato farms. The shell road between the farms took them to the empty grass parking lot. A small brown sign read Pond Hawk Environmental Preserve at the trailhead into the 200-acre county preserve that bordered Loxahatchee National Wildlife Refuge, the very northeastern edge of the everglades.

"Thanks for coming along," Samuel said.

"Yeah. Is your ankle all right?" his son asked.

"About 95-percent."

On the trail, the son noticed his father's three-quarter steps and the dissonance to his stride. A tiny warbler flickered across the path and into the shelter of a scrub oak.

After hiking down the overgrown trail a good ways, they sat down on a hollowed tree trunk. A wild muscadine bush shaded them.

"I came out here every morning and would pick one of those flowers for your mom when she was in the hospital," Samuel said. "Every morning that I could I'd come out. There was another field of them by the lake, even bigger than this field. I kept bringing the flowers. She would smile like it was the first flower I brought her and we were eighteen again. After a week though I noticed the dried flowers were gone from the nightstand beside her hospital bed. I figured the nurses threw them out."

His son's boots swept the sugar sand. He was glad the boy was there.

"Sometimes I don't know how I will get through the day." He rubbed his palms over his closed eyes and opened them. "I haven't been much of a dad lately. I'm sorry for that."

"You did better than I would have in your shoes."

"I didn't even go to your college graduation. I couldn't. I sat in the truck in the parking lot watching everyone else walk by with their parents and family. I got there early so I could talk myself into it I guess. I just couldn't get out. I wasn't ready to be around people."

"You were in the parking lot?"

"That's as far as I got."

A checkerboard of sun and shadow spread across the sand, and a pondhawk dragonfly circled low.

"When I went in to pack up her things and clean the room, I found an Altoids tin in one of the small drawers. It was full of dried flowers. Had to be twenty of them crammed in that tin. One of the nurses told me they tried to throw out the flowers, and that's when she started to hide them. She got the tin from another nurse and kept every flower in there."

His father got up and put his floppy, long brimmed hat on. They hiked the open hammock through pale green and paler green in every direction. When they got to the lake, everything looked the same and smelled the same.

"It's been a while since you've been out here," his son said.

"Yeah."

The county had built a small platform where you could walk up along the edge of the lake, but other than that it was exactly the same.

CHAPTER TWENTY

November 15
Solitudo County

The first winter storm came early, bringing a foot the week after they closed the gates to the road at Overlook Pass and up Highline Ridge. The snow was fresh and soft and higher than the tread on his boots. It would solidify overnight if it kept on snowing and the temperature dropped down as low as he thought it would. When he walked up, Tift was leaning against the old shed next to the far corner of the pen. It was a big pen, an acre and a half fenced, but it must have been a prison cell to a wolverine.

She leaned against the aluminum siding of the old shed, looking out into the pen.

"Hey," she said when she saw Thomas.

"Hey."

As the two figures stood there, making noise, the animal wanted to run. Run to the big pines. Run so quickly that nothing would be able to track her. But there was the high fence on four sides, metal wires hard, unbendable like a trap.

"Has she tried getting out?" Thomas asked.

"No, not anymore."

She would run as fast as she could. Across the miles in this new territory, snow accumulating on the open prairie earth, running towards the pines over there, shadows and no sound under the big trees within sight.

"How long will they keep her?"

"Till spring probably," Tift said. "They said she only ate once, more than a week ago. They put something out every afternoon and she won't touch it. Soon they'll put out mice or a rabbit to see if she can feed on her own."

"She can probably smell our scent on the food."

"Yeah, that's what I was thinking."

The wolverine backed further into the pale winter shadows in the far corner, where she could try to hide in the still, cold winter air. The one taller than any other moving figure, with his familiar scent heavy. The two figures weren't moving. They were not the ones who brought the food, their odorous, bad food. Along the fence, behind the trees, they could not see her, although they could probably smell. Low in the shadows, between the maple and pine, snow coming down and cold, windless air, the animal crouched still. Displacement from a home of dark earth and thick tangled roots is a pain that gnaws like the rusted steel locked down. Yes, the wolverine would run herself free if she could. Run despite the stump of a leg severed. Run and run and run until she lost her way from this pen. She had a wide space to go.

"We fit her with a GPS collar. She's W-43 now. But I call her Acacia." She looked out into the pen and she looked at Thomas. "You think it was the Centur Corp. men?"

"I know it was," Thomas said.

Tift didn't say anything. She just looked back out into the pen.

"You said she had a den on Highline Ridge up on the northern edge?" Thomas asked.

"Yeah," Tift said. "She had to of. We found all these tracks, and none of them left the area."

"That's right where they're fixing to build a road," he said.

"They can't build a road through there."

"They're going to try like hell."

"What are you going to do?" she asked and stood there for a long time waiting for him to answer.

***

In the cold, snow-covered space north, almost north to the twin peaks of the lower Selkirk Range, between the ridge and Wolf River, the geophysical surveyors embedded another geophone into the ground. Twisting and hammering, they inserted their instruments into the earth.

Only one of the men wore the Centur Corp. uniform shirt. The others wore flannel layers and wranglers, and one wore a Packers sweatshirt. They listened to Toby Keith from the jacked-up Expedition.

Their geophones hooked up to cables that ran back to the truck.

Winter Beach

Samuel still remembered how the bluebird came flying right over his head. Running as fast as he could, Sammy chased that small bluebird through the open field behind the houses.

The bird would fly low and land down in the tall grass, and when the boy got close, it would lift off again in a flash of bright blue wings. The boy ran towards the creek, and the bird flew across it in a patient measured flight towards the edge of the pine and scraggly oak forest. The boy took off his sneakers and socks and waded across the muddy, unmoving water, stepping fast in the deepest parts because he knew there were snakes in the water. On the other side, he sat down in the sandy soil to put his sneakers back on. The bluebird was gone, and Sammy felt a sadness without the musical, chittering song of the bird taking flight.

Sammy walked west towards the pines, looking up waiting for his bluebird, but there were only the branches and pine needles. He looked back, and he could no longer see the creek he crossed, so he tried to remember which way it was. Everything was covered in that fading sun of dusk. The boy thought about heading back, but he kept walking. He passed a rusted fender and what was left of a tire from an old car someone had dumped back there a long time ago. The boy came far into a part of the forest where he had never walked before, and he just wanted to see the bluebird again.

Samuel still remembered how the bluebird came back.

The bird flipped off a low branch back into the air, blue wings and amber throat shined brilliant in the light that sank through the branches. The bird hovered in the air, its wings beating a thousand times a minute, or more, if the boy could count exactly. It circled around the light in the air, and flew back to the branch, before flipping back into the air. All of this was an explosion of amber and blue color blending together.

The boy would later read in the birding guide that his mom got for him that the bird was flying for insects it would catch in his small beak. He would read that the bluebird, like other gnatcatchers, would sometimes switch his tail swiftly to scare up hidden insects, especially at dusk.

The boy looked up in awe. Back on the branch, the bird switched its tail quickly from side to side, and then it flew away.

The boy followed. He felt the rush that comes with not knowing what was going to happen next, and he kept his eyes on the bird flying low and then up between two small oaks. He stayed close, trying to be careful not to scare the bird off as it landed in another oak, this one with branches that shut out the light. The boy looked up in the branches, but the bird was already gone. The clouds moved above, moving steady. The boy sat down in the grass and dead leaves under the tree. He held his thumb and finger up as a window into the clouds, which moved an inch a minute. The boy waited, but nothing moved besides the clouds and wind and a bee that landed down on the yellow-orange flower growing from the crumpled leaves. It got cold. The boy picked up a leaf and threw it up in the air so that it drifted down in the wind.

He first thought of the story he read about a far away place a boy had escaped to. Sammy sat there under the tree. It was an old oak tree, low and wide, its branches dark with moss and lichens and twisting out from the thick trunk.

The boy heard the chittering song again, and saw his bluebird, joined by another one that was paler, with more gray and only a blue tinge on the wings, perched up on the highest branch. "There you are," the boy said softly.

The pale moon had risen through the oak branches, and the boy knew his mom would be looking for him, so he turned to head back, and he walked though the forest, past the rusted remnants of the old car, across the creek, and through the open field behind the houses.

When he was crossing the field, he heard his worried mom calling "Sammy. Sammmy!"

As he walked up to the back door patio, his mom asked where he had been.

The boy said he was lost.

That summer he started drifting even deeper in the woods. His mom didn't say anything when they started to have dinner a little later each day, as long as he walked up to the back patio before darkness. And some nights even if they already ate, she would keep dinner warm for her son and sit down with him while he ate.

He walked out to the patio and put on his worn sneakers as soon as he finished his chores in the house, and put on his worn sneakers and ballcap. In his knapsack he had everything he needed— with crackers and an apple in a plastic bag, the binoculars he bought for two dollars at his neighbor's garage sale, his Swiss army knife, and an extra pair of socks rolled up at the bottom of the pack. He would venture out with his knapsack. He would soon learn the rich call of the eastern bluebird, the robin, cardinal, gray catbird, Carolina wren, and the blue jays.

One afternoon Sammy was out where the oaks grew way past the creek when he saw the black clouds coming. He could see the rain coming down in the distance. Those black clouds moved closer, and he hiked fast back towards the creek, but he didn't get too far before it began to rain. He realized he was still far from the creek. The rain slanted down through the gray sky and soaked his shirt. The boy was scared and cold, but he had found the big oak. He sat down against the tree. He sat there against the bark etched deep with wrinkles against his back and with his head just under the lowest branch. The rain beat down on the branches above. He tried to think of the story he read about the faraway places the boy had escaped to.

Sitting under the branches, the oak looked huge, with so many branches tangled above, like the scary place where the boy in the story had gotten lost. But that place was imaginary, and this wasn't.

Sammy thought the rain would have to stop. It just rained harder. He would have to cross the creek after dusk. The boy had known the storms that would come in from the coast of Florida in the late summer, but he didn't know it could rain like that. He felt like he would cry, and he didn't care what anyone would think about that. All the rain in the clouds was emptying out. He sat under the tree, and he could feel the tears. But when he started to cry, he realized it was a useless thing, and it wouldn't stop the rain.

The boy looked up to where bluebird had been perched, waiting out the rain just as the boy had been. The bird perched on a branch and shook his soaked-through feathers, not more than ten feet from the boy. The boy smiled because right then he loved that tiny bird. The boy and the bird waited out the rain, and it kept coming down.

CHAPTER TWENTY-ONE

December 1
Conservation Area 2A, North of Wilson Sanford National Forest, Idaho

It had dropped down to ten below by morning, icing over the snow under his boots. He was trying to find the shortest route back to the truck when the sound of movement snapped the quiet in the forest.

From up here he could see the black Ford Expedition, down on the eastern edge of the pass. They're fixing to try to put that pipeline down through Shadow Pass, Thomas thought. They think no one will be here to see anything out here, at least until the weather breaks. No one to see their lifted Expedition and the deep tracks in the snow.

They've probably been out here all winter surveying, and they've been damn smart about not being seen. They'd been up here, but they had been damn smart about it. But this far north and west? Beyond the boundary of the conservation area?

This land can be ragged, and it can be bitter cold. It's right in the middle of the biggest wild, undominated land in the continental United States, where the wind comes straight down from the mountains. There ain't a soul for fifty miles, except Thomas and however many men came in that jacked-up SUV. There it stood, down in the pass, tall on 40-inch mud tires, pulled off into a clearing a few yards from the fifteen-year-old lodgepole pines where they had cleared the forest twenty years ago—before it became part of the forest's conservation area. In all modern history, someone always saw this land as a forest to be harvested, and they came with the machinery of their time to try to get as much as they could. There won't be any harvesting today, Thomas thought.

Oscar was right. Thomas remembered how Oscar had told him they were fixing to build a road up through Highline Ridge and along Wolf River all the way up to Rilla Lakes. First a road. And then a pipeline from town that'd have to cross the river. Thomas remembered when he'd said there wasn't no way to do it, and how Oscar said they were sure as hell gonna try. Just north, it's a straight cliff down to the river. This is where they'd have to do it. The pipeline would have to go right through here all the way down the pass. This is where they'd try.

With a pipeline here they'd be able to pipe out gas from most of the forest, including the three large tracts of conservation land.

Them and their pipeline can go to hell, Thomas thought.

It began to snow again as the truck drove down and west into the pass, black smoke shooting from the exhaust and the tries kicking up the mud under the ice.

They can build a straight line to hell, Thomas thought.

They drove that jacked-up SUV right down the steep side of the pass. When he saw the angle they took up the other side, he knew they'd get the heavy Ford stuck in the snow and ice. He knew they'd get stuck good.

Even with tires that tall, without traction, you're not going anywhere. "You ain't going nowhere," he said aloud.

He felt the cold on his neck and face. Thomas stood there looking down, and he thought for a moment that he should go and try to call it in. He told himself, call it in, as the big tires spun in the snow. The tires spun in reverse, spitting snow and ice, and then spun the other way, as the driver tried to rock the SUV free, the heavy truck unmoving, buried up to the axles.

Somewhere in the time divided by seconds that followed, he knew he would not go and call it in, and he walked to the truck. He felt it get colder. But the blood under his skin burned despite the cold wind. How could anything but hatred exist once he saw the inevitable future? Fifty miles of hell bent pipe from the pass up to Rilla Lakes, one long road cut through the forest, trucks carrying greed's machinery, grunting, scraping trucks.

Every white pine ripped up to clear way for the machinery encircled by signs saying that this wild land is now off limits. "Flammable: Compressed Natural Gas Pipeline" a sign would say. They will stay for 15 years, maybe longer, just long enough to up and leave when there is nothing left to harvest. Invisible carbon flowing into Wolf River and her arteries, Rilla Lakes full of fish rotting in the water.

Acadia would already seek another home—a place to try to build a den. Even if she tries, where would she have left to build it?

Nowhere left, nowhere saved.

Then the others might see what they've done.

Maybe he wanted them to know what it felt like to be cornered, trapped. So he slid the scope and barrel steady and slowly towards the target.

Through the magnified glass, the clouded dusk and the snow made a gray static.

Thomas could faintly hear them yelling, and one of the men stepped out and walked around to the winch on the front bull bar.

That wind blew cold. The man had the winch and was anchoring it to a pine, and he was saying something to the other men in the Expedition. In two minutes time, they would be winched free, driving up over the western edge of the pass.

Maybe he would fire a shot into the sky. Maybe he would shoot the warning shot. But he didn't aim for the sky. When the first shot hit rocks under the snow, he saw the fear in the men's eyes, and his heart rejoiced in the fear they felt.

He put four more rounds in. He kept his finger brushing against the hard metal of the trigger, and he squeezed it again. He aimed to the right, blowing out the rear tire in that Expedition. It didn't look so big now. He saw the man with the tattoos looking out the window, looking back up to the ridge trying to see where he is firing down from. The son of a bitch knows there's no sheriff's deputies coming round. Long before they do, he'll know something else. Thomas had two more rounds left. The tattooed man was turning his head all over like a scared animal being hunted, trying to see where the shots were coming from.

***

Winter Beach

Samuel pulled the December 1972 issue of *Avian Ecology and Studies* out from the shelf where it had somehow landed between the issues of *Computer Review* and *Comics and Animation*. In boxes and shelves all around, old journals and magazines stacked high. Here was all the material that no one thought was important enough to leave out on the first floor or save online.

He sat down at the only table between the shelves and a dust-covered empty glass case that probably once held the library's small collection of first-edition books. It was a dark mahogany table nicer than anything upstairs. The polished wood was covered in dust and the smooth lacquer scratched from years of use. Samuel wiped a clearing in the dust with his sleeve. He put his glasses down on the table and strained his eyes to read the print. There was one light barely shining from the other side of the tall shelves.

The journal had reprinted Murphy's 1962 photo in the lower corner of the detailed account of a sighting ten years later at Rilla Lakes. As Samuel turned to page 213, a quote from Robert Cushman, renowned ornithologist, stood out: *"I can still recall the cinnamon flash under the wings."* The editors ran one of the old Audubon illustrations that showed the white and cream belly and the cinnamon flash under the wings. Samuel bent over the desk trying to read the smaller print under the illustration when he heard the thick-soled, shuffling feet.

"Sorry. No one usually comes down here," the librarian said as she flipped a switch on the wall, turning on a single white light above. "Better?"

"Yes, thank you."

When the shuffling footsteps were gone, and the hum of the air-conditioner was the only sound, Samuel looked down again at page 213. He skipped down three lines to where he had left off.

The morning dawned dry and cooler on March 7, 1972. It was exactly ten years and one day after Murphy had taken the last undisputed photographs of the Northern Stilted Curlew, and a young Robert Cushman, just earning his reputation for his studies of the migratory patterns of shorebirds, was out studying the American golden plover. When Cushman saw four larger shorebirds fly up from the south and land in the shore vegetation in the distance, he initially thought they were Whimbrel. Samuel pushed his chair closer to the desk and leaned over the dark mahogany to read the next few lines.

"It was unusual I thought for Whimbrel," Cushman wrote,

"to travel so far north this early in the year, and two of the closer birds looked slightly taller than Whimbrel. But even through the compact binoculars I was looking through, the birds appeared to be Whimbrel. I walked a few yards closer, from where I had a clear view of two of the birds closest to me in the lower sandy marsh shore.

The birds did not move, further causing me to believe they were Whimbrel. Then suddenly, as I must have gotten too close, two of the birds flew off directly towards and then overhead where I stood on the rocks. I can still recall the cinnamon flash under the wings. I took note of the flash under the wings, which was more light pinkish on one of the birds, as I watched the pair fly closer. I also noted long, more decruved bills, the dark brow markings, and the cream-colored bellies. I knew these were not Whimbrel.

It is worth noting that the Stilted Curlew shares the same migration route each year with the American golden plover, of which I had observed several dozen on the shore of the southern reaches of the Rilla Lakes. This being early spring, it was more probable that a very small flock of Stilted Curlew would be found this close to the Canadian border than it would be for Whimbrel.

As an intriguing sidenote, Smith has reported that a comparison of dates and migratory patterns leads to the conclusion that the southward-migrating Stilted Curlew and American golden plovers were most likely the shore birds to have attracted the attention of Christopher Columbus to nearby America in early October 1492, after 65 days at sea out of sight of land.

Was it true, Samuel wondered, that the species of bird we had to thank for the discovery of America has been vanquished by the very desires that had led an explorer to find this uncivilized land.

***

Stalking the birds, which had circled above and landed about forty yards off, Cushman couldn't believe his eyes. Through the binoculars, he watched the shorebirds. They were almost certainly Northern Stilted Curlews, a species even then believed by some to be extinct.

Then I heard the call, a call I had never heard before. A call that sounded like a faint *tee-teeee-teeee*. *Like it came from a songbird or warbler, but softer, muffled almost. And then upon alighting, one or more of the Curlew gave another call. A variation of the same call, but more audible.*

***

Samuel re-read the last three lines before he closed the journal and picked it up from the scratched and dusty varnish surface. He climbed the stairs to the main floor and walked to the copy machine.

CHAPTER TWENTY-TWO

December 4
Solitudo County

Williams, the lawyer, walked up to the small table anchored to the concrete floor and took a seat on the other side of the table. Snow melted on his jacket.

"It's still snowing?"

"Yeah."

Thomas could only tell it was still daytime from the high, narrow window. He would wake in the middle of the night and wait for morning to show through the window.

"I'm not going to ask what you were thinking. But shit, Thomas, you should have called it in."

He couldn't find anything to say, so he looked up at the lawyer.

"I can't represent you, not while we are fighting the drilling legislation."

"I know."

"I'm recommending a colleague. If you want, she can come by tomorrow."

"Okay."

"She's good. So listen to her. I've already told her about—about your case."

"I will," Thomas said.

"I will call her when I leave."

"I decided I'm going to resign," Thomas said.

"Okay," Williams said.

Through the window he could see the light fading.

"That can help. Listen, you might not think this. But you've got a shot at starting over. It won't be easy. But Susan will work on getting witness statements from the Centur Corp. men. The more we pressure them, the more I think they won't want to talk. I have a suspicion the company don't want the whole world knowing their plans for a pipeline through two conservation areas yet."

Thomas nodded.

"No witnesses, no case," the lawyer said. "The best thing you can do now is send a letter to Eckhert, he still runs the forestry service right? And Susan will help you draft it."

Thomas nodded again.

"Is there anything I can do?" Williams asked.

Thomas handed him a small folded paper with Tift's phone number written on it. "Can you call her? I left a note for her on the kitchen table. She has a key. I'm worried about Japhy. She might have to take him for a little while."

***

Some wading birds spend two-thirds of the year in migration, either on wintering grounds or in the air, in flight. Some species such as pelicans and storks are daytime migrants. Other waterbirds fly through the night when conditions are ideal such as cooler temperatures and calmer air.

The Northern Stilted Curlew is a nocturnal migrant. This allows the Curlew to cover more ground, gliding with the springtime northern fronts as their tailwind.

In the 1950s, Swedish ornithologists Eleanore Lonnberg and Lars Kurlmein demonstrated that night-flying birds have the ability to navigate by the stars. During their studies, Lonnberg and Kurlmein observed several migratory flocks of Northern Stilted Curlew. The team was able to identify the star patterns the Curlews used when navigating at night. It was assumed that the North Star was important as it is fixed in the night sky, but the surprising result was that the birds instead used star patterns within about 35 degrees of the North Star. The birds called to each other throughout the night to help keep their flight formation and avoid collisions.

CHAPTER TWENTY-THREE

April 3
Conservation Area, north of Wilson Sanford National Forest

Far from her home, W-43 began tracking north over the folds in the earth. There were stars bunched in the sky, and the snow-melted field was still frozen under the top inch of soft thawed soil. There was the thick covering of pine needles and then some of the dry, crumpled leaves.

She yelped, just once, and kept her nose to the earth. Time was measured by space crossed, cold wind, and that song of night wind that changes and pulses but doesn't let up. Turned loose, she kept her nose to the soil and pine needles, and she trekked back towards the tangled roots and dark-soil earth down in the river gulch.

She had trekked for a long space through the night, and it was just barely morning when she smelled something. A light flashed.

The cold wind came down into the low, interior space of the gulch. So close.

"Go get Jim. Hurry. Tell him to bring the rifle," the man wearing the Centur Corp. hardhat said.

The wolverine stopped. She looked at the men dividing her and the den on the other side before she continued towards them. The man fired a single shot into her chest. The animal's body remained in the bloodied earth until someone came by that afternoon and put her in a black trash bag and dropped it into the bed of a truck.

CHAPTER TWENTY-FOUR

November 2
Solitudo County

It was a new November, and the looks didn't bother him that much most of the time.

Thomas was getting used to it. The looks. Most of the time, they were more discreet. They wouldn't stare so much as they'd look inquisitively, letting their eyes linger. Most of the time at the grocery store or post office, they would wait to talk until he walked past. Some of the real good ol' boys, like Wilby, would stare him down and start talking about him just before he was out of earshot. Thomas placed the three grocery bags on the passenger seat and got into the old Toyota pickup. It took two cranks to start. He'd have to fix that starter. Stop putting it off.

He drove thirty in third gear until he got out on Route 12. A Silverado at the gas station bore the sticker GET THE GAS. SAVE OUR ECONOMY. The Silverado's owner must have put it there a while ago. There wasn't any need for bumper stickers anymore.

Thomas had waited forty nights for the morning light through the window when the lawyer came in with the news that the state had dropped the charges. It was a Thursday. She told him that he wouldn't need to go to the courthouse that morning. The lawyer put the folder down on the table, and he thanked her.

He was living in a singlewide plopped down on the three acres purchased years ago as vacant land when he was still working for the park service. After taking out ten grand for the singlewide and a thousand for that Toyota with too many miles on its second engine, his savings account has dwindled down to almost nothing. He stocked up on groceries when he could. His tattered boots probably should have been replaced a few months earlier. He was starting to feel pebbles and hard ground through the worn soles. But it was a new November, and that was something.

***

He'd only had two clients so far, lawyers from Ohio, friends of Williams. The two men spent a full weekend fishing the river with Thomas. The one who talked a lot surprised Thomas with his beautiful casts and when he rinsed his hands in the water before he held the first trout so the trout's fragile skin wouldn't be harmed by the oils on his hand. It was the small things like that, which sometimes surprised Thomas with people. The lawyers left Thomas a two hundred-dollar tip, on top of the hundred-dollar-a-day fee.

Taking out-of-towners fly fishing had its perks, and Thomas thought he could make a go at it. He hoped he could if he just stuck at it. Only time would tell.

Tift had been coming to see him more and more. Since she was the first woman whose company got better over time, he was trying his best to keep her. Thomas knew how complex someone's story could be, and he wasn't one for generalized biographies. But he knew how his sounded.

And there was the morning when Japhy started barking loudly and trying to scratch through the door. There was the sound of tires peeling out, and whoever was outside was gone.

When he walked out he saw the truck was leaning to the driver's side. They slashed two tires, and they probably would have gotten all four if they had a few more seconds. On the hood they spray-painted: FUCKING TREE HUGG. Japhy had scared them off. It had to be more than one guy. He had plenty of guesses who.

Tift was scared. But she stood with Japhy, petting him and trying to keep the dog calm. She told Thomas he had better call the cops just in case.

The deputy remembered him.

"About what time did it happen?" the deputy said.

"This morning," Thomas looked at his watch, "a little after eleven."

"See anyone leaving?"

"No. There's some tracks. Looks like the newer all-terrain truck tires, Yokohama or—"

The deputy walked over to where the tracks were. "Could be any truck tire," he said.

"They're wide," Thomas said.

"Yup, wide. You going to file a claim with insurance?"

"Probably not."

"I'll fill out a report just in case," the deputy said and walked back to his patrol car. He came back in a few minutes and handed Thomas the narrow sheet of paper. Under incident, the deputy had checked vandalism: two slashed tires and hood spray-painted. The deputy didn't say anything else.

A week later, Tift told him about some red-headed high-school kid she overheard defending Thomas to his friends outside the diner, and Thomas wondered if it was the same kid he came across camping in the park two Octobers ago. The kid who had wanted to see a Wolverine. The red-headed kid was the exception. Wilby would be talking now to anyone who would listen, saying what most thought. When Thomas Wayson's name was mentioned, it was a safe bet it was bad. There are a lot more popular positions to hold in northern Idaho than that of a rogue park ranger who shoots at the gas men, who tries to stop the first sign of progress in these mountains in years.

Thomas hadn't really known Wilby well, but the old man had been friendly enough. But after Wilby read about what happened, that changed. The one thing clear was that Wilby made no effort to disguise his hatred. And it got worse after his youngest son got a job as a generator tech with Centur Corp.

***

Her Jeep was there when he got to the end of the long, narrow trail.

He told her the day before that he would cook dinner. It was going to be a surprise—bass on the grill, zucchini from the garden, and pasta with fresh tomato sauce. As he walked up to the door, he heard paws scratching and scurrying on the laminated floor. He put down the groceries, Japhy trotting in circles, his tail knocking chairs, the legs of the table, the fridge, and anything he circled past. She landed a kiss on Thomas's cheek in between the dog's enthusiastic greetings.

The dog squeezed between their legs.

"Before I forget, some guy called for you, Samuel Leaton. That's the birder isn't it?"

"Yeah. When did he call?"

"About an hour ago."

"What did he say?"

"Not much. I told him you'd be home soon. He left a number."

CHAPTER TWENTY-FIVE

March 4
Somewhere over Missouri

The half moon already floated over the clouds, and the photographer of birds looked out at the ice particles and the fading light of dusk, and the farmland far below.

He had the warm three-way jacket rolled up under his arm, and the warm sleeping bag under the seat because he didn't want it to get lost or damaged in luggage. The pilot came on the speakers and told them it was forty-one in Boise, and Samuel knew it would be a good twenty degrees colder at night up in the forest.

The photographer of birds recalled the sounds he'd heard—three years earlier—in the South Carolina pine bluff. He didn't know if he would ever hear that call again.

***

Solitudo County

Thomas sat at the table with the bundle of dubbing and the tiny fish hook in the clamp. The dog lay under the window half asleep, his eyes half open to the sun. Thomas added the blue-gray wing wool to the Dusty Miller. He'd try this one on the clear streams that fed from the lakes into Wolf River.

Three thousand bucks was a lot. Thomas thought about that. That could pay the next two payments on the trailer, and some new gear. Thomas was never one for those $450 Orvis setups, but that's what the clients expected, and it'd be good to have one.

When Samuel told him that the magazine wanted to hire him as a guide, and that was how much they'd pay, three thousand for three weeks give or take—about-normal for a backcountry guide for that long—it didn't change how much it was to him. It was money he really could use. Maybe he could get that Orvis superfine touch outfit that he had seen last time he was in Henry's Fork. The guys he took out fishing would notice that. It was the little things like that that they would notice. Thomas thought about how maybe next time he went down to Henry's Fork, he'd talk to Frank about adding him to the guide list they kept at the store. It would help out a lot, but he didn't really expect it.

CHAPTER TWENTY-SIX

March 6
North Bridge, Wilson Sanford National Forest

North of the old logging bridge, they took the old two-rutted logging trail another half mile until it faded into tall grass between the needle-straight forests of second growth lodgepole pines. A mile further, the footpath went up between two lodgepoles.

After the first cutback in the trail they heard a loud bang like the sound Samuel heard that first March he hiked north into the forest. The ground vibrated. Another loud bang broke the silence.

"Are they testing?"

"They're setting up to drill."

"There isn't even a road."

"Across the river. Probably two miles off. They'll be two more there. They'll pipe everything out. Pipe it cross the river and down towards town."

Directly to the east the bang came again, followed by a sound more muffled, a constant, clanging, droning noise. There was more banging like someone throwing chains against metal.

The two men didn't say anything more, and they hiked away from the banging noise. After they had hiked through the morning, the river was far behind them.

Thomas carefully lowered his pack when nine hours later they reached the foot of the first ridge. He took out the water and the topographic map. Samuel never thought he really looked the part of the forest ranger, even in uniform. Not that he couldn't be a ranger, but he looked like a man out on a long-distance-hike-through. And now here with his dark flannel, and that worn panama hat that was tearing worse along the top and taped along the seam where it was coming apart, he looked like a man trying to get away from something, or hiking to find something.

Thomas unfolded and laid the map down.

Since the last time the men saw each other, Thomas had shaved his beard, and Samuel had grown a full one. They hadn't spoken since Samuel was up nearly two years ago—a long two years ago.

Samuel had read about what happened, and had wanted to help Thomas in some way. He knew the articles only told one side of the story— a vague outline of events, the list of charges, Thomas's resignation, and then finally three months later that the charges were dropped. But those three articles posted on *The Independent-Tribune's* web site didn't answer why. No reporter would know that. Samuel thought he should make a call, do something. But what could he have done. So he read the articles. And he hoped for the best in a bad situation.

Until that Thursday the lawyer came in, Tuesdays and Sundays were the same for Thomas. He did think about the Curlew, and whether the photographer of birds had gotten his photograph. He knew that was unlikely, that the shorebird had probably slipped away. He had seen firsthand the chemical runoff that would ensure our destruction of the last remnants of wilderness would continue into another century. He saw little reason for hope.

***

The banging sounds were far behind them after some time, and here the only sound was the light wind. Samuel's legs wanted to keep moving because he had gotten into that rhythm of a good hike, and he felt like he could keep going.

"We're on Kootenai land," Thomas said.

"We're still going north."

"Yeah. We went too far west. We can cross back before the forest."

Samuel knew Thomas meant the old growth buttressed against the foothills. The forest was many miles away still, but he could see it, the blue shadow of the pines rising up before the folds of the lower Selkirks.

There was no trail on the map marking the way up through the old growth white and sugar pines, to the south and east of the foothills, and further north-north-east up through the giant two-thousand-year-old, moss-covered red cedars with trunks more than five-feet across and then the marsh of the first glacial lakes of the Selkirks, and the clear streams that flowed into Wolf River.

"We can stop and check the GPS when we get to the forest," Thomas said.

"Okay."

They continued north-north east.

From this distance, the white pines and cedars looked like the same pines of the forest behind his house where as a boy Samuel chased the bluebird, although he knew these pines ahead where four times as tall. For a moment, hiking into the woods to try to find the Curlew was as simple as crossing that creek and hiking out, watching, and listening, stepping softly and waiting for a soft call in the distance, trying to spot movement where the wind turns every pine needle. For a moment it was as if the Northern Stilted Curlew was probably not gone forever.

***

In the morning Samuel was up boiling water from the jug Thomas had filled at the river.

"I guess I slept in," Thomas said when he sat down to put his boots on outside his tent.

"No, I couldn't sleep."

"Not at all?"

"Maybe an hour or two."

"You'll sleep good tonight after the hike ahead."

Soon they were climbing higher, two figures, small and slow moving through the shadows of the forest, zigzagging their way up the wrinkle in land. Still below the timber line, the pines grew wide.

"This is only the foothills," Thomas said. "More like the toes."

"One hell of a toe to climb," Samuel said.

The two men stopped, and Thomas took his water bottle out.

"You didn't make it out this far last time did you?" he asked.

"No," Samuel answered.

"We're making good time."

The shadows of the pines grew larger until all light was gone in the forest.

The river was far behind them now.

***

March 8, Conservation Area, just north of Wilson Sanford National Forest

The foothills of the lower Selkirks—which were really just toes as Thomas said—were behind them and to the west, rising up almost directly above them, and the wide glacial lake ridge opened to their north. The Selkirks was behind them. They had hiked nearly fifty miles along a trail so faint they couldn't trace it if they looked back. They had at least five more miles to go, but here Samuel could see the place he'd been thinking about and had read about and seen photos of. A hawk glided above the closest lake, a sun-lit speck circling low in the light gusts. The hawk, a roughie, was hunting, drifting in the wind and for a moment even appearing to fly backward along the shore. After the tall white pines and the cold forest of the giant cedars, and then the smaller cedars and pines, and the maple hammock, the lake plain was astonishing. Wide open and light and flat, it was the opposite of the forested lands they had just hiked.

They stood on an open windowsill with a clear view of the glacial lake plain. The lakes stretched as far as he could see, clear water and surrounding marsh, a mix of blue and green Samuel had never seen before. The rock ledge shore of the southernmost lake showed almost white, and sheets of clear ice floating on its surface caught the sun's glint. Under that tall grass there would be all the bugs and fallen crowberries in the decomposing muck that a Northern Stilted Curlew could eat if one were to land down after its migration back home.

CHAPTER TWENTY-SEVEN

March 9, Day one at camp

Thomas began gathering downed branches. Before dusk, he had a small stockpile of pines and some of the cedars that the wind had knocked down, and he was tucking pine needles and dry grass under the triangle of the driest branches. Shielding the small flame from the wind, he put the match to the dry pines, which began to crack with fire before the match burned down to his fingers. He shifted one of the branches so more air got inside the triangle of branches. As the flames kicked up, he lowered a few more of the dry branches onto the triangle. The luxuries of the first night at camp waited on two of the big snag branches. There were the two good-sized crappie that had to be close to three pounders, marinating in the pan with garlic and peeled orange, and the wheat pasta, can of diced tomatoes, the dry basil for seasoning the sauce, and of course the fifth of whiskey.

Samuel took another sip from the whiskey and handed it back.

"When I was a kid, I loved fire, like any kid, you know," Thomas said. "I would practice starting fires with my Swiss Army magnifier."

"Yeah, I remember those."

"One weekend I started this blaze of a campfire right next to my fort in the backyard. I didn't think I could get a fire going like that so fast with the little magnifier, and I fed it with pines from a big ol' pile of branches I stacked." As Thomas talked he shifted another branch into the core of the fire. "Within two minutes the pines were blazing, and the fire was right up against my fort. It was so close the paint was crackling, so I went and grabbed the garden hose, but by then it was too late."

"It caught on fire?"

"Oh, yeah. I was spraying the fort, and smoke was everywhere. Our neighbor came running up and went inside to tell my mom."

"Did you put it out?"

Samuel took a good drink. The almost-full moon floated in the sky, painting the clouds a purple-tinged gray. He took another drink and felt the wind.

"I remember just watching how fast the fire spread. It looked like the sky was on fire. It was a good thing the neighbor had called the fire department before he ran over."

"Oh, no. How old were you?"

"I was ten or eleven. It was my mom I was worried about. My father wasn't around too much." He took another tilt from the fifth. "I guess he had given up on us by then. And I just didn't want Mom to think I did something that stupid. That's what I kept thinking about. That my mom would think I had let her down the way my dad had."

"It could have been worse."

"Yeah. She made me sit down in the kitchen. I though she was going to tear into me. She was quiet for a long time, and then she told me that she could tell I learned my lesson."

Samuel passed it back across the fire, the orange and blue flames burning good, and Thomas took a tilt from the fifth.

"You know, I'm damn glad you haven't given up on the Curlew," Thomas said.

"Well, I guess some people can get an idea in their head and it just sticks."

Thomas put another pine down, and the fire snapped and burned bright blue.

***

In the morning, Thomas walked out from the pines towards the first of the lakes. He wanted to get a line in the water, and he wanted to leave the photographer alone, let him make that hike around the shore of the big lake. It was even further than it looked, and he knew Samuel would be out for some time.

He felt the kick from the coffee. Up here there wasn't no electrical miles or anyone with an iPhone. Just a hundred miles of lake plain and marsh and tributary creeks and the mountains in the distance to the west and the pines and cedars to the east standing over their humble camp on the gentle sloping ridge. He felt good about the trip, and he hoped the weather would hold out the way it had so far. There was a lightness to his step now that he didn't have the heavy pack filled with three weeks of supplies including the ten-pound bag of rice, lightweight single-burner stove and propane can, water purification tablets, the necessary bars of multi-purpose soap that could be used for bathing, dish cleaning, and laundry, sleeping bag, tent, and the absolutely necessary cloves of garlic, small jar of honey, the dry basil, and the fifth of whiskey for the first night at camp.

He had read up on the Northern Stilted Curlew after Samuel told him he was coming back up. He knew now about the disputed sightings, about the disappearance of much of the shorebird's wintering grounds, about the eradication of the crowberry plant. He knew the odds had been stacked against the Curlew for a long time, and he didn't think the photographer had any false hope either. But hell, everything worth anything is a long shot, and he really was glad Samuel hadn't given up on the Curlew. If he didn't look for it, who would? Maybe, just maybe, that beard of his would bring good luck for Sammy the bird photographer.

When Thomas reached the shore, he kept walking until he saw the reflection of three good-sized crappies.

He cast the line out and watched the wet fly sink, and he waited, letting the fly drift a foot from the bottom, until a crappie came up and nudged the fly. Then he saw it, coming from the submerged snag branch, the largest trout he had ever seen, swimming up to the fly with her big rudder tail switching slowly, in no hurry for anything. The crappie took off, and through the clear shore water over the rocks, the pink fins and yellow belly of the cutthroat flashed like metal. She was in full spawning colors, the mark under her jaw was bright red, and she had to be thirty inches. Big soft belly and hundreds of tiny spots along her flank, and those beautiful red marks. Thomas reached up with his free hand and tipped two fingers to his hat to the monster trout that shot off with a flicker of that rudder tail. He watched the silt wake left behind as the trout swam off.

***

March 10—Second morning at camp

Thomas went out from camp back towards the shore where that big spawning trout had shot off into deeper water. Not too far from the shore, he saw something partially buried in pine needles and soil. It was part of a small sculpture that looked like it was made of some kind of stone. It was dark, submerged for a long time in soil and water. Thomas reached down to pick it up and saw it was a wolf figure, attached to a long piece of half-rotten wood. The wood was cedar that had been adzed and smoothed, the remains of a dugout canoe that the Kootenai had left behind a long time ago. It began raining.

***

It was a mist rain that evaporated as soon as Samuel felt it on his arm. A small chickadee, a chestnut-backed, hopped around the rhododendron. The small chickadee sang out a soft chuckle, that's what it sounded like, as if the tiny bird was laughing softly, enjoying its breakfast of the almost-invisible insects.

The chickadee flew off, and Samuel stood looking out over the rhododendron that grew up along the open scrub just above the lake plain. Beyond the rhododendron, he could see miles of marsh that stretched clear up through the creeks flowing down into Wolf River.

Before the sun started pouring into the lake plain, Samuel set the Nikon on the tripod. He sat in the soft rusted, brown cedar needles, leaning against the cedar, the smooth peeling bark cold against his back.

His plan was to wait. Wait, with the feather cedar needles under his boots and the camera on the tripod. The morning was still cold. It might break into the forties. And the sky was a shade of blue he couldn't describe in his head or notebook, a shade of blue as blue as the everglades in the early morning, a blueness that poured over the lake plain and the pines. He plucked a tick from his shin. It was relatively large, as far as ticks go, so he didn't worry much about it. He fiddled with the Nikon till it was just right on the tripod. He put his knee up and leaned back into the cedar, and he waited as the morning went by, the coffee thermos within reach. The chickadee came back, joined by another, both chuckling and circling through the open scrub overlooking the lake. When the chickadees flew off for good, there was no sound.

The only other outside visitor they'd seen had come the morning before, the small plane sputtering through the sky, its noise faintly funneled to the ground. The pilot was soon gone, leaving no evidence of the mechanical drift that was present moments before.

They too would have to leave the blue mornings of this open lake plain. They would hike out where the trail is barely visible to head home. But there was still time here yet. Nine more days, eight of those mornings. The sun kept pouring down into the valley, and the southerly wind picked up, the first sign of a front moving through.

CHAPTER TWENTY-EIGHT

March 11, just below North Bridge

The thunder came from the machinery down on the other side of the river. There were more of them. In the morning, more of the odorous, loud men returned, and the thunder started again.

The old wolf circled, below was the river and the slate shore, then the straight pines and the bigger pines where it was all shadows, and the empty space right up through the pines. The wolf stopped because the thunder came again. The thunder reverberated, shaking ground and sky, and below the machines moved like it was their land. Up on the flat rock above the river, the wolf crouched as the machines smashed and drilled into the dark earth. The wolf crouched low, a sting of confusion echoing across the gulch, and he looked north.

The men inside the trailer sat under a map taped up on the paneling. The map showed an angled line of dots right down through Solitudo County. The line ran along the river through the middle of the map, each dot marking where Centur Corp. would drill through dirt and rock. The line ran along the eastern edge of the river, starting at Big Fern Gulch, all the way north to

Rilla Lakes, before it circled around the lake in another line marked by more of the dots.

The old wolf, tired and hungry, lay down to sleep, and in the morning, north beyond the Solitudo County border, the wolf trekked, past the lands it knew, through the soft, decaying pine needles, the ferns and bottom woods. Above the branches of the tall trees clashed in the wind. There was a rhythmic steadiness in his steps through the tall, wet grass and the pine needles. The old wolf had survived rifle and bow and the coldest winters when he would hide carrion in the icy soil and pick from the splintered bones. Spring would always come, ice melting and the mice out in the fields and the fish soon spawning in the river, and then the long sun of summer months. But the wolf will not make it one more summer.

The wolf passed another metal sign not yet rusted like the others.

CHAPTER TWENTY-NINE
March 12, Day four at the camp

After they finished eating the white, flaky fish and the rice on the tin plates, Thomas took another sip, and when he leveled the bottle Samuel could see there was less than an inch left.

"You read bout what happened?"

"Yeah I read the article in *The Independent*," Samuel answered.

"I know they ran a few."

"I saw two or three online. I remember reading the story when they dropped the case."

"Shit man. I don't even know why it happened. And I tried to figure it out," Thomas said. "I've tried to."

"It's done," Samuel said. "They dropped it."

"It was right before the first hearing. I was getting ready for the courthouse when my lawyer walked in and told me. They would have liked more than anything to send me behind bars for a few years," Thomas said. "But they had to withdraw their testimony. A case like that would have just gotten in their way."

"Yeah," Samuel said.

"They don't need to hide anything now. They've got all the permissions and permits they need to drill right up through the forest. This summer they will drill sixteen holes. I guess it was just a matter of time."

"There has to be something—"

"They say there's an estimated ten billion worth of natural gas under Highline Ridge alone. It was stupid to think anything would stop that." Thomas took a drink. "To think one man could change things.

"Saw on the news before we left," Thomas continued, "They showed the President talking about Solitudo County, about the gas boom coming here, he called it the clean energy tomorrow project—or some shit like that. Everyone wants to drill this land dry. They want to turn the national forest into a factory. I'm not enough of a fool to think they won't drill. But why can't they just leave this patch of land? Just leave it wild. Once they change it, there won't be no going back to the way it was."

"What about what the lawyer from AWL said?"

"He tried," Thomas said. "Took it to the courts, as high as they'd listen."

"They're going to appeal though?"

"Appeal? No one is listening anymore. Naw, no one is listening. It makes me want to – drink this damn bottle and another one. It's a lost cause now, Sam.

"Sometimes I think maybe one day people are gonna say 'Why didn't someone just warn us, why didn't they stop us from drilling and bulldozing everywhere, try to save a few places'," Thomas said. "The ones who won't listen will be the ones to say why didn't someone warn us. Maybe then they'll realize: Hey, there was a warning, they were trying to warn us, but we called them fucking tree huggers, we ignored everything they said."

***

That night before the wind came, Samuel thought about what Thomas had said. He thought about what the drilling would do to the marsh, to this last possible breeding ground for the Curlew. He thought about the lightness of birds.

Then the wind came, steady at first followed by the cold rain and the relentless wind. The wind came straight through, and the sounds crept as in a dream until the rustling vinyl of the tent and the whistling tugged Samuel from sleep. He slid on his boots and went outside. Darkness was all there was. Branches snapped. There was no light from the sliver moon behind cloud cover. The wind, a scratching whistle, wouldn't let up.

The wind and the shadowy outline of the pines were the only things perceptible, and the wind began ripping down like an arrow from the hills, and Samuel had to lean into it to stand up. He heard pine trees swaying into each other.

The wind tore Samuel's vacated tent from all but one of the anchors, before subsiding back to a whistle. Thomas came out of his tent bootless and moving quickly, and the two men pinned down the tent. There was a rip in the side of the tent, but nothing that probably couldn't be repaired with duct tape and a patch of vinyl. With a ringing clang and crash, the wind knocked over the propane stove and something else. About fifty yards away it snapped a pine, the top half crashing down to the ground. It started to calm and then picked up again, blowing harder than it did before. The wind did this for most of the night.

In the very early morning it was still windy, although a different, lesser wind, and tiredness was all Samuel felt as he lay in his tattered tent hoping he would catch maybe an hour of sleep. It was one of those mornings camping when you wish you were in some fireplace-warmed living room with your coffee and a good book to read and no appointments to keep.

***

Three hours after sunrise, the wind had died down some and Thomas went down to the shore. He thought maybe he'd be able to cast down shore but the line looped back in a circle. It was too bad too, because a trout rolled out of the water lunging after an insect. Thomas thought he heard splashing and movement on the rocks, and he looked north. About eight hundred yards from where he stood, the bear was on the shore. Fishing. And having good luck at it. Water pouring down from his thick fur, he had a good-sized rainbow in his mouth. The grizzly was a big boy, larger than the one Thomas saw a few springs earlier just south of here, this one nearly five feet tall on all fours. The grizzly dropped the fish down on the shore and dove back into the water. Thomas was downwind, and the bear didn't smell or hear him. A flock of birds lifted from the water just north of the fishing bear, the birds taking flight and tucking their legs in unison. They flew overheard and alighted south on the shore, their long legs now sunken into the mud, the bear paying no mind to anything but the fish in the water.

Thomas laid down his rod and backed up the same way he came. At camp, Samuel was trying to get the propane burner on the stove lit.

"You've got to see this," Thomas said. "Bring the camera," he added, which was unnecessary because Samuel was already reaching for it.

They were a quarter-mile from the lake, downwind, when Thomas stopped. Samuel aimed the camera's trusty 70-300 mm long lens.

But when he looked through the viewfinder, it wasn't the bear though that caught Samuel's attention. He focused the lens to 266.0 mm and the birds came into closer focus. As soon as he could make out the larger golden and black specks, he knew they were golden plovers. There were forty of them, or more, down a ways from the bear still pawing the water. Stilt-legged, skipping clumsily around everywhere along the shore, the plovers high stepped out into the water to pluck mollusks or whatever else they could find from the water, before running back to eat their catch.

They were whistling their beautiful, melancholy song. One scrappy guy fished up a crayfish, twisting his head to shake the water from his catch four times longer than the thin bill it was clamped in.

As Thomas and Samuel got closer, the bear scampered off. Samuel noted the plover's beautiful, melancholy song. The sight of the plovers, along with the dry, calmer air following the front, meant that this would be perfect flying weather for the Curlew, if in migration. With the footsteps of the men getting closer, the whole flock flew off and alighted a hundred yards north, where the plovers resumed their search through the muck. That evening, Samuel was trying to get the small propane burner lit to see if it would work. "Man, we don't need it," Thomas said, and Samuel saw him looking at the contraption with contemp. "You're right," Samuel said.

***

The following morning, the weather had changed again. There was almost no wind, what birders sometimes call "absolute calm," a rare condition that only comes maybe once a year, after a certain kind of front that pushes warmer air north. Usually migrating birds won't wait for absolute calm because they would never migrate if they did. But sometimes during this time, shorebirds that migrate at night will fly through the morning and part of the day, also, because the flight conditions are ideal.

The idea that bird migrations proceed according to the weather is by no means new. The biologist Wells W. Cooke noted that in spring birds prefer migrating in warm weather. At the time, this concept met with strong disfavor by many top-ranking ornithologists. Wetmore and company supposed that birds were driven by an irresistible migrational urge to arrive at the breeding grounds by certain days on the calendar, and they argued weather had little impact.

Then in the 1930s, a pilot with Eastern Air Lines who often observed birds at three thousand to ten thousand feet, wrote "to a bird on the wing, the wind is a vehicle or means of transportation. The bird will fly with the wind and always with the least resistance. It is the air that goes places and the birds go with it." The science has become more precise since then, and there is a group of ornithologists who study weather radar data and satellite imagery to try to pinpoint when a specific migratory species will land down in a specific location, sometimes within the exact day and fifty miles of touchdown. But the formula for such predictions is complex, and sometimes the prediction is more of an educated guess that happens to match the migratory will of the species than an exact calculation, or at least that's what Samuel thought about it.

But he did know that absolute calm could last a few days, or even up to a week, and it was during these ideal conditions that the Curlew could be flying through both night and most of the day. These conditions, along with the plover sighting that morning, could mean that the Curlew was coming back home for the spring.

That night, Samuel looked for his sleeping socks so he wouldn't dirty the inside of the sleeping bag, and as he got into the bag where it was warm he was reminded of a book he'd read when he was a kid. Although he was anxious and ready to see what the next mornings would bring, in the warmth of the sleeping bag he finally began to drift to sleep. A small, helpless bug, hovered low, and flew into the corner where the camera was stowed neatly, along with the lenses, and extra batteries that had become so heavy and almost uncarryable during the last few miles of the hike to the camp.

During the night the wolf howled his long unbroken howl.

From a moan to low-pitch howl, and finally the long modulating song, the wolf called from the north. Then the dark night was quiet again.

***

"Did you hear the wolf?" Thomas asked over coffee mugs in the morning.

"Yeah, it was close."

"Up there," Thomas said, "up in the hills to the north. It sounded like only one wolf though—calling to himself."

The Northern Stilted Curlew was forefront in his mind. Maybe the Audubon painting or maybe Murphy's grainy photographs. For four years, he has seen the colors of this image, and he cannot just set it aside as an old relic of something extinct and gone from of our own time and history and our damn forgetfulness and greed. He was glad Thomas was here. It could be no one else. Thomas knew what it meant to keep on going. He knew.

As he ate his oatmeal, he had an idea. He would climb up to where the wolf howled. From there he would wait for distant figures in flight that might drift from the south.

CHAPTER THIRTY

March 15, early morning
Conservation area north of Wilson Sanford
National Forest

From here he had a wide-open view of the lake shoreline where the plovers skipped their skips, their spangled backs reflecting the morning sun, and all the way south to the Selkirks rising over Kootenai Land.

Samuel stood up here where the wolf had howled. The pines of the north reflected in the lakes, and directly to the south, he could see the tents and a dot where they burned their fire. The sun on his shoulder, Samuel set up the Nikon on the tripod and whistled a James Taylor song to himself. Through the telephoto lens he saw three larger, darker stilted legged shorebirds mixed in with the plovers.

Even though the birds were still too far for a very clear shot, he was thinking they might be Whimbrel—that species of shorebird that is nearly identical to the Northern Stilted Curlew from a distance.

The Curlew's bill is slightly longer and it has a more distinct brow marking and different underwing coloring. The cinnamon flash underwing would be the most discernible difference, but only visible when the Curlew was in flight. The shape, flight pattern, and other features are as close as the nearly identical grasshopper and Henslow's sparrows in the same field. Only those ornithologists who have studied the two birds can distinguish the difference—between the sparrows, and between the Curlew and Whimbrel. He was not certain, and mostly it was the laws of probability that told him it was probably Whimbrel.

But it was strange to see the Whimbrel this far north this early in spring, and they sure did look like the Curlew from that distance.

The birds flew up from the reeds along the shore and headed in the direction of where Samuel stood, calling as they flew. Samuel stopped and turned to the calls of the three birds, tuning in to every note he could hear. The call of the Northern Stilted Curlew was something he may have heard only one time back in the pine bluff in South Carolina. But he remembers that call, and this was not it. As the three birds flew overhead that sunny morning, they sang loudly, clear and rapid, a series of seven notes of the same high pitch, *pip pip pip pip pip pip pip*—a sound unlike the soft, melodious, and varied three-note whistle of the Curlew.

As they approached, he knew for sure. He knew that it was Whimbrel flying overhead.

Through the long lens, the tan, almost cream underwing coloration, and the shorter bill were clear. He pressed the shutter release quickly, five or six times. They were spread out so he could only photograph two of the large shorebirds in the same frame. He zoomed it to get another shot, close up, of the last one as they flew further away. There was no cinnamon flash underwing.

The birds had surprised him when they lifted in flight, and he had been slow to get the camera focused on them. He knew several of the photos were no good. When he got back to camp he viewed the best, clearly-focused shot, zooming in so he could make the photo of the last Whimbrel. It was solid, but it was not his sharpest capture.

They really do look alike, he thought to himself. One could mistake this species for the Curlew if the bill was just slightly longer, the eye buff somewhat more pronounced, and if it had the cinnamon axillars.

He took one more look at the best photo, and he thought about it. Samuel thought about how they could *fake* it, fake sighting the bird.

It was a dangerous, bad thought, but that didn't stop him from thinking it. After half a century without a confirmed sighting, a Northern Stilted Curlew photo would change everything. He didn't want to think about this. Knew he shouldn't. It was his reputation on the line. There was more than that on the line. But he did think about it, the thought not lasting long enough to unravel before he was already trying to get it out of his head.

***

That night the full moon burned, and the old wolf continued north, beyond the second of the big lakes. The wolf made a path between the tall grass and the hardwoods that border the edge of the lake plain.

In the early morning, the blue-white moon still hung over the pines when Samuel stood outside the tent, sleeves rolled up and holding his coffee, his other hand in his pants pocket. He looked out at the moon and the motionless clouds in the calm sky. If done right, it would be impossible to tell.

There is a way to do it right, he thought, but he couldn't do it, not perfectly. You had to be careful of certain things. The bill and the eyebrow buff would have to be edited. Retouched really. It was the underwing that would have to be altered, requiring multiple minor changes to the original digital file. The thing to watch out for is light. Someone can tell if a photo was altered by distortions to the way natural light flows. Even a slight change must take into account how the light appears in the original photo.

There is a new technology that Samuel read about on one of the birding forums. Using this technology, they can scan the JPEG file and tell if the photo was edited. But even the best expert can only tell if the file was altered, and not to what degree. So if he admits to changing the color scale to contrast the bird from the cloud clover in the background, it won't be a surprise if anyone determines that edits were made.

The last photo would be the best to work with. It only showed part of the underwing coloration, and the lighter tones that any ornithologist would know belongs to the Whimbrel—not the Northern Stilted Curlew. That would be the tough part.

He knew Ryan could do it—It'd stop the drilling. If it was done right.

Samuel would have to call in the information to the state's bird records committee for the rare species list. That'd be the first step. Renee would get an article out in the next issue of the magazine, but even before that every birder and ornithologist within five hundred miles would rush to the forest. Then there would be a meeting of the rare records committee to vote on the sighting, to collect documentation, and finally vote whether the evidence was credible enough to establish the specific identification of the species. But before that, there would be enough Tilley hats and binoculars walking the forest to get the attention of DNR.

Is there a difference between really finding it, or making the world believe it exists? When it comes to saving this wild land, it might not make a difference if it's fake or real. It might be the last hope.

***

Karia painted her nails. The jade-green polish faded as it dried on her nails. The last time she had painted her nails she was fifteen, almost sixteen. She didn't think he would notice, but she wanted to look nice, a little different, and nice. She added the thin layer of polish, and waited for it to dry while the floor cleaners slid tables and chairs downstairs and the news recap of the Republican presidential debate droned on the television.

Soon she began to fall asleep to the news. The television droned on, and she could hear the floor cleaners downstairs, still sliding tables and chairs.

***

Samuel had spent the night wondering if he should tell Thomas, and when morning came, their eighth morning at Rilla Lakes, he decided.

"We could fake it," he said.

"What?"

"Fake seeing the Curlew."

Thomas turned away. He didn't like it.

Samuel tried telling him how they could do it.

Thomas shook his head.

"It'd stop the drilling," Samuel said. "Finding the Curlew would stop it. Just the hope that there was a small population holding on."

"I don't know."

"It'd be my reputation. I'll say I saw it. I'll write an article about it. My editor wants to believe the Curlew exists more than anyone else. Maybe Ryan could work on the photo. He can do it."

"No one would believe us anyway."

"They might. The Curlew is here, I believe that. We would only be faking the proof. Even if we really did see him, right off, there'd be a group that says it's impossible. They'd demand proof, and we'd have to fight our way through it. No one would believe it until we didn't give up on it."

"Fuck, Sam. You're gonna make your kid do that?"

"I don't know if anyone would believe it. If they did, it would change everything. You don't think it's worth a shot?" Samuel said, but as he asked it and thought more about how they would have to do it, he began to think they shouldn't. He couldn't do it alone, and he didn't want to drag anyone else into it.

Thomas looked down. No, he didn't like it at all.

***

In the morning, he took his gear and headed down to the lake without saying much. His boots crunched over the pine needles as he walked through the shade of the big pines. On his third cast a cutthroat took the hook and twisted and shook free not far from shore.

Thomas was glad the small trout had broke free, but his anger and tiredness returned when the ripples cleared. The lake was a shade lighter than the green-brown tall grass growing up around the snag branches and the rocks on the shore. The waters would be a waveless, clearer light some mornings when the sun was at a certain angle, and it would be an amber tea color where the cedar pines fell along the northern shore. Yet whatever the shade of the water, the lake always had a clarity to it, even where it ran deepest.

He thought about the old dugout he had found half-decomposed back into the earth, and he thought about the Kootenai who had inhabited this canyon range for thousands of years. This lake plain must have looked the same up here. But how long would it stay? Soon they'd bring that line of shit-brown rigs, groaning and spitting exhaust, and then they'd lay the pipeline. How many holes would they drill in the earth? Would we have to try to remember what the open sky looked like, the untainted river and the green marsh, the rolling pine-tree covered foothills where no roads cut, the spring rhododendron in the open scrub, this last refuge for the cutthroat trout, the wolverine kit, and the grizzly cub?

There would be no escaping this future set forth in motion already, he thought. Something right under his feet was already cracked way down under the surface, where the gas company executives, Governor Scottson, old Wilby, and a judge had started to chisel and bang until it cracked. It was a fissure they shattered into the earth, and the crack would only grow. There are some scars the land can't just grow over. There are some scars that will slowly tear deeper.

Thomas knew Centur Corp. wouldn't be satisfied until they had control over all the land here, protected or not. Just the way the timber companies wanted all of the land north of Salmon River.

***

Samuel had been quiet, and it was unsettling. Or maybe it was just unsettling that a photographer of birds would want to *fake* a photo. Thomas didn't know what the photographer's true intentions were. What his real reasons were. But, no, Thomas didn't like it, no matter what the reasons were.

He just didn't want to think about it anymore, about what is right or not—he'd been through that shit before.

He just wanted to be home. Home in his singlewide, with the linoleum that was two shades too close to snot green, with the thin glass that didn't keep the cold out, with no cable or TV and with the damn bedroom carpet an even uglier color. But it's home, Thomas thought, where he can eat a good dinner and where he can sleep next to Tift and shower in the morning with those four minutes of hot water. Where he could wake up without fighting. Make breakfast while she still slept, with Japhy his good, loyal mutt curled up in the kitchen, patiently awaiting that piece of bacon.

What damn good are a home's four walls, though, when your real home around you is being torn to pieces?—When you make that home an island so you can ignore the big rigs driving further north—the clanging, stamping, the reverberating booms of the machinery testing for more gas under the surface, the yelling and cussing, day and night. You may have become an island from many things—but you're no island from this land. Maybe you have one more chance to do something.

CHAPTER THIRTY-ONE
March 15
Winter Beach, Florida

She awoke and began to erase the nail polish, first rubbing back and forth, clumps of jade green peeling off, then scraping with her nails down to the cuticles and picking off what was left. Her fingernails still felt like they were heavy with a layer of scales.

She went into the bathroom and let the hot water fill the tub. Hair over her left shoulder, she lowered into the burning hot water, the odor of the bath salts in the damp air, and she leaned back, as if she was an old lady at the dusk of the day, with only the hot water and bath salts to look forward to. The water turned rose where her cuticles bled and stung from where she had scraped down and filed too far. The hot water swallows her shoulders as she submerges lower. When she stops breathing under water there is no time. But she knows it will return. Time is a scar. Her scar has only faded lightly. She can still feel it, vivid, even as she drowns out time. She touches it under the water that's no longer burning hot to her skin. She can feel without time, or maybe because of the absence of time, but what would it feel like to know there was no more time anymore. She sinks to the bottom of the tub and holds her breath.

***

Karia. Karia, her mother called. Come back. *You're going too far,* she called to her daughter. Okay, the girl nods, pedaling back closer to home. Her mother smiles for the last time.

Karia. Karia, what's gotten into you. Snap out of it. No, you can't stay. We're going back home. Now.

Karia. Karia, you little bitch. Be a good girl. A good, nice bitch. Karia, you good girl, that's good—

CHAPTER THIRTY-TWO

Four days later
Solitudo County, North Bridge

The men had hiked for a long time, and when they could see the narrow bridge over the river, the mountain wind picked up for the first time in days. It rolled the tall grass down along the river. Then another sound came above the wind. At first it could've been the wind knocking a snag pine, but the sound was steady and more mechanical, and louder until the first of the big rigs came up the old logging road. The rig drove up onto the narrow bridge where someone got out and unlocked the chain and dropped it down in the dirt.

There must have been twenty of the rigs that followed, all of them ascending north towards Shadow Pass and beyond that Rilla Lakes. Flatbeds loaded down, dump trucks, and a water truck, each painted the same faded brown with black fenders and wheels. CENTUR CORP. tattooed across the back of the water truck with an American flag painted underneath and "Get R' Done" in small square letters. The forest service had given them a key.

A minute after the trucks and the noise were gone, Thomas stopped and looked down at the river, the expression on his face matching his old hat, worn thin and tattered like it would have ripped in half with another good wind.

"Okay. We'll do it," he said.

Samuel couldn't find the words so he didn't say anything.

"There ain't no other way," Thomas said.

"I'm not sure it was a good idea. It was—

"We need to do it right, like you said."

The two men kept on walking. Thomas felt the exhaustion and anger tearing at his nerves, and that was probably why he changed his mind. No, he thought, that was not why. He changed his mind because there was no other way.

***

One week later in Winter Beach

It was that time when the lunch crowd had cleared, and there were only a few left sitting outside. The hair salon owner leaned back in the sun smoking his cigarettes and talking to everyone who came past. As they did everyday, Hank and his owner were sitting at their table, opposite the salon owner.

It was quiet inside. Ryan walked to his table like it was the first time he walked in. Four days earlier, he had told her about the phone call from his father, and how he couldn't stop thinking about it. How he told his father it was the craziest thing he had ever thought up, and that they couldn't do it anyway. How he couldn't stop thinking about the phone call though and what his old man had said, and how Ryan just should have told him he wouldn't do it, period. How he told his father it was crazy and stupid, and he would realize that soon enough, and how every time he goes out there he gets into some kind of trouble. How he hadn't talked to his dad since.

"Why do you think he asked me?" he said to her when she took a seat across from him.

"Who else can he trust?"

"I started it. The file."

"You're doing it? I thought you couldn't?"

"I can try."

"You sure?" she asked.

This son of Samuel Leaton, so tired eyed, long haired, with his grin somewhere between caution and courage, he would fight.

He would fight for his father, for the Curlew, and he would deceive the world. She knew he could. He would fight for her. She knew he could. He just couldn't save her. But she would love him.

CHAPTER THIRTY-THREE

April 1

Renee sat down at the coffee table to her breakfast with the TV on like she did every morning. But she never paid much attention to it. The morning talk show was just background noise in the house as she had breakfast and checked emails. The weather was on.

She sat down to her fruit and toast and turned on the laptop when she noticed that she had a missed call on her phone. It was when she checked the voicemail and heard the words *Northern Curlew* and *Sighting* together that she spilled her coffee all over the table. Ignoring the coffee dripping from edge the table, she listened to Samuel's message twice.

***

April 4, in the back of Elk's Club Lodge 501, Solitudo County

The committee chair spoke from the makeshift dais of two long tables set up in the back room of an Elk's Club Lodge.

"Samuel, let me first say we appreciate you taking the time to be here. Have you ever been to one of these before? Well, we're a pretty friendly bunch, but there are a few rules we've got to follow. We have to record the proceedings. Do you agree to let us record this? Okay, is it working?"

Another committee member, a woman who was the youngest looking of the five, was trying to get the voice recorder to work.

"I think you have to press down that button," the committee chair said, "hold it down. Okay, now let the record show Samuel Leaton has granted permission for an audio recording of this meeting, and that we provided him with a copy of the committee guidelines."

They had set up several rows of seats, but there were only two other people in the room, a man with thick glasses sitting five feet behind Samuel and a reporter in the back row with a laptop beside her.

"To be honest I had given up on the Curlew," Samuel said. "Like most, I guess."

"But a few weeks before my trip up here, I read Cushman's account. I read it in some old journal at the library. I think it was *Avian Ecology*."

"Cushman's sighting—it was in 1972?" the woman who had started the tape recorder asked.

"Yeah. March 7, 1972 in the National Forest. I think his account was written several months later, after the actual sighting. Well, I remember how Cushman wrote about the differences between the whimbrel and the Northern Stilted Curlew. How he had noted the subtle differences in his field journal: the long, more decruved bill, the dark brow markings, and the cream-colored belly. But what stood out was the cinnamon flash underwing. I remembered that description."

The reporter was typing on her laptop.

"Shelia printed this map with the GPS coordinates that you gave us. Does this look right?"

"Yes."

"And there was another birder with you?"

"Yes, but he was at the camp."

"Okay, so you were the only one to sight the Curlew?"

"Yes."

"We've all seen your report and the photo. Some of the committee members had comments or questions, and I'm just going to go down the line. Tim is our expert photographer, and he had a few questions for you."

Tim spoke with a soft voice that was barely audible over the clicking keys from the reporter's laptop, "Okay so in your report you noted that three birds flew overhead. How close were they flying. To each other?"

"They were fairly close, less than five yards, but with the long lens I was only able to get two in one frame," Samuel said.

"How many photos did you capture?"

"Several. But that one photo is the only one that came out clear enough."

He asked if Samuel could submit the other photos, and he said he could but that they were not good quality, that the first photos he took were not in focus, not until the last shot.

**

April 5

A small but eager group of birders gathered outside the ranger station at Wilson Sanford National Forest.

They checked the batteries in cameras, and made sure they had their extra layers for when it got cooler. A retired biologist named Patrick and his granddaughter from Las Cruces slipped past the group and drove their Jeep to the end of the park road and parked it at one of the overlook areas three miles before North Bridge. Armed with a map Patrick had studied the night before, binoculars, a Coleman tent, a pack full of water, sandwiches for dinner and snacks, they hiked into the forest, hoping to be lucky and fortunate and prepared enough for the slim chance of spotting the Northern Stilted Curlew. In his pack, Patrick had a photo of the Curlew he had printed from the online database. Four decades earlier, he had known the then-young biologist who had sighted a pair of the Curlew, but he knew that finding this species now would be a miracle. He was cautiously heartened by the recent news of a sighting in this national forest. But it'd be highly improbable, even if the sighting was correct, for someone to cross paths with the Curlew a second time. But he didn't have anything better to do. His wife had convinced him to bring their granddaughter along for the trip. He was happy the girl had left behind her comfortable room and a weekend movie date and decided to come along.

The retired biologist and his granddaughter hiked for a long time and ate their sandwiches before they camped in a clearing. In the early morning, Patrick woke up to the noisy pair of Chestnut-backed chickadees that matched the brown bark of the pines in the morning light, and soon the girl woke. They headed back south after they ate the last of the granola bars and Patrick made some tea. There were the plovers flying overhead, a bald eagle circling, and nearly twenty of the Townsend's warblers chirping and flickering.

There were no Curlew.

***

There was activity at the ranger station back at the entrance. A dozen with binoculars were standing by their cars and SUVs. A U.S. Fish and Wildlife Suburban was parked next to two white vans, and a trio of the birders were talking to one of the forest rangers. The reporter for the *Independent-Tribune* pulled up in her Saab. She fished around the Saab for the printed copy of Renee's blog post and a clean notebook from the ones strewn on the passenger seat and across the dash.

Two hours earlier when she told the city editor about the story, Carolson didn't believe her. "You've got to be shitting me," Carolson said when the reporter told him about how she found some blog post from a birding publication about this single photograph—which is an "incredible discovery" according to the blog post that the reporter printed so the editor could read it:

> We need to spread word about this. If this sighting is proven to be authentic, it may be one of the most incredible sightings in the past fifty years. It is of the upmost significance that these rare Curlews were seen smack in the middle of gas country, not even five miles from a dozen more proposed hydrofracking drill sites. The Northern Stilted Curlew is one more species that will be extinct in my children's lifetime, unless we act now...

"Are you thinking what I am," the editor asked his reporter.

"Yeah."

"Call your DNR contact," he shouted, even though he was one desk away. "See what the hell this means? We need to know if this could mean a delay in the drilling."

"It isn't good news for Centur Corp." the reporter said.

"Call them too. But call DNR first."

The reporter had picked up the phone and called one of her contacts, the DNR guy, who was driving up to Solitudo, but no, he didn't know much, except that the state's rare bird committee would vote on it, deciding if the sighting would be entered into Idaho's rare species database. He told her that everything depended on the vote.

CHAPTER THIRTY-FOUR

From RENEE'S BIRDING BLOG, posted 4:32 AM:

Habitat Preservation Holds Key to Recovery for Curlew!

April 6| By Renee In newest posts, conservation, photography comments (84)

Government agencies spent more than $5 million to try to save the dusky seaside sparrow in the early 1980s. But it was too late for this small shadow of the tall grasses that once sang its husky-voiced song throughout the fragile marsh environment of coastal Florida. The Space Shuttle Program's massive coastal development had already gobbled up most of the duskies habitat, and the too-late effort to set aside traces of land couldn't sustain the population. The Dusky had already been decimated to fewer than one hundred.

Every single day matters when we are trying to save a species vulnerable to extinction—such as the dusky seaside sparrow. And preservation of lands in peril is often the only way to save some species in peril. The **recent sighting** of a pair of Northern Stilted Curlew in Solitudo County, Idaho, in the northern reaches of Wilson Sanford National Forest, has renewed hope for this cold-weather shorebird that has largely been forgotten. It is a hope as light and fragile as the shadows flying through the tall grass.

We can watch another species slip away, or something can be done! Centur Corp. has already started drilling, and the efforts to open all of Wilson Sanford National Forest and surrounding lands to expansive gas and oil drilling is a looming threat that grows by the day.

The glacial lake plain in the northern stretch of this federal preserve in particular could be one of the remaining necessary breeding habitats for the Curlew. Over the past forty years, nearly half of all known sightings of the Curlew were reported within one hundred miles of the borders of the pristine 800,000-acre forest. The habitats of glacial lake plain and mountain prairie are one of the last islands of habitat hospitable to the crowberry plant that the Curlew relies on as its main staple during breeding.

The Northern Stilted Curlew needs Wilson Sanford National Forest. The glacial lake marsh within this forest is one of the last areas of habitat suitable for the Curlew's breeding grounds. Just one bird, one rock-solid sighting, can kick trigger the Endangered Species Act, if it is properly enforced.

This National Forest has to be protected—as it was intended—in order for the Northern Stilted Curlew to stand a chance. This is not silly, unrealistic thinking. It would not be the first time in recent history that a species in peril was saved by looking at the issue through the lens of land conservation. It will, however, be a formidable battle in a state that is becoming more dominated by the interests of natural gas companies such as Centur Corp. We must remember that in history, sometimes, to the surprise of many, the birds win.

The very first national wildlife refuge was set aside under President Teddy Roosevelt's administration, specifically to protect nesting heron colonies from plume hunters.

We all know about the Northern Spotted Owl and the efforts to protect the old-growth forests this species relies on. After years of fierce fighting between quixotic conservationist and logging company lobbyist and private landowners, the US Fish and Wildlife Service updated their conservation plan to create a 10-year plan that set aside a network of 133 owl conservation areas totaling nearly 6.4 million acres of federal land west of the Cascade Mountains' crest in Washington. The goal of the conservation areas is to support a stable number of breeding pairs of northern spotted owls over time and allow for their movement across this network.

In a lesser-known story, further south from where the losing fight was fought to save the duskies, in the 1960s, another small group of quixotic conservationists led the fight against wealthy developers who wanted to build condos and a tourist mall on the seven-acre Elliott Key north of Key Largo. They planned on building a causeway across Biscayne Bay, right through a roseate spoonbill rockery and breeding habitat for shorebirds such as the threatened Wood Stork. Today, thanks to the effort of three unrelenting conservationists, Elliott Key is protected within the boundaries of Biscayne National Park. Let us learn from history. Let us call on the Department of the Interior to suspend all drilling activity until we can study the Northern Stilted Curlew and its presence in northern Idaho. This species has been largely ignored for the past three decades, and the sighting in Solitudo County could be the impetus for truly necessary scientific study. But first we need to ensure the Curlew's precious habitat is protected in the spirit that this land's original use was designated.

I have attached one of Samuel Leaton's photographs of the Northern Stilted Curlew below.

***

Winter Beach, Florida

Ryan stood by the counter drinking down the last of his coffee. She watched him holding onto the mug. She looked out the window behind him.

The early sun slanted in through dust, and she felt it on her arms.

He smiled and kissed her goodbye and headed out the door to the marina. She moved quietly after he left. Her silence astonished her as she picked up his mug and put it in the sink, and as she navigated the small apartment, drifting around, reversing back towards the kitchen like an apparition. She opened the window, and the sun and breeze sank in.

She would miss the smell of coffee when she opened the canister, and she would miss the disorderly space of the small kitchen. A moth flew in the window with the breeze. The plain white moth navigated the dust like a half remembered dream.

She let water fill the old mug from the café with a chip on the handle, and she watched the moth circling nervously. The moth flew into the main room above the couch and the small TV and into the kitchen, landing on the table. Under the light, Karia could see that the moth was not plain white or pale gray, but streaked with the palest shades of emerald, pink, and turquoise, the colors breathing against the dusty pale light of morning. The moth flew up and circled, flying one last flight before it found its way out the window into the morning, trailing colors that faded into the silence.

CHAPTER THIRTY-FIVE

From RENEE'S BIRDING BLOG, posted 12:15 PM:
CURLEW UPDATE!

**April 9 | By Renee In newest posts,
conservation |comments (152)**

I want to update everyone with some great
news!

The Department of Interior decided
yesterday to enact an **indefinite ban** on all
"gas drilling, exploration, and production"
within the boundaries of the Wilson
Sanford National Forest, and the
surrounding one hundred miles of land,
directly bordering the national forest. I just
read **the press release** from the office of
Frederick Grimes, DOI's Secretary of
National Lands, announcing this
moratorium.

The Idaho Rare Bird Committee met last
week, and Grimes asked the committee
chair to send a copy of their report once it
was completed. Here is **a copy** of the IRB
report. Within two days of receiving the
IRB report, Grimes issued the press release
announcing the ban on drilling. His
decision to issue the ban was thoughtful
and forward-thinking, and I wouldn't
hesitate to call it heroic.

***

That night, no spotlights burned through the half-cleared fields crisscrossed by a thousand dozer tracks, and no one worked on the unfinished pipeline that reached halfway up to Rilla Lakes. In the morning, the first of the big rigs hauling machinery began to leave the forest, the wheezing diesels retreating slowly from the foothills and through the river valley, and rattling across the bumps and dips in the muddy access road from Shadow Pass. The Centur Corp. men closed up the trailer with the map tacked on the wall. They loaded up generators and machinery, and locked what they left behind so no one would steal anything, and they left a maze of pipes like a den of fragmented snakes uncoiled.

On the way out, one of the rigs hauling a dozer had a blowout, shredding the left front tire on a root. The rig blocked the narrow access road, and three other drivers pulled off to wait for the repair truck to come out.

"Why the hell are we moving out today?" the driver of the rig with the blown out tire said.

"They don't know how long it will be," another driver answered.

"If I'd known one bird could stop the world, I'd a shot it out of the sky a long time ago," the first driver said.

"Shit, Jim," the second driver said. "You ain't gonna find no Curlew."

"I'd blow it into extinction for good," the third driver said.

"You been working on your shot?" The men laughed. "Even Jim's a better shot than you."

"I'm serious, man, shoot that bitch with a .22. They can't trace spent shotgun shells."

The men laughed and spit, as they stood next to their loaded-down trucks waiting on the muddy road.

***

Somewhere north of Rilla Lakes

The wolf moved, with his muzzle low to the grass and the blue-eyed Mary wild flowers that just bloomed, following his path along the pine ridge that rose higher above the creek and river waters funneling down into the plain. He stopped when he heard a shriek of a call. It was a lone bird, but it was not a hawk nor harrier.

The bird glided against the drifting clouds, tilting occasionally from side to side, and as it passed above, the rising sun lit the bird's red streak under its wings. The bird flew on its way, singing gently now. The wolf stood still, smelled the air as the wind picked up again, and the bird shifted, turning back and flying into the wind, its shadow sailing over the taller grass before landing down. The wolf leaned forward into the wind that stirred the pollen and the faint, warm sunlight. Beyond the wind, the bird landed down at the edge of the mountain prairie. It scuttled through the grass scooping plump berries from the earth.

CHAPTER THIRTY-SIX

Loxahatchee National Wildlife Refuge, Florida
Another September

Samuel's boots slogged through the wet sand that only two days before was dust dry. The sand absorbed the rainwater that hadn't streamed down into the canal. He hiked, and a merlin called from the early morning darkness. The sun splashed across the marsh. There was not a single ripple on the water, and no movement in the sky—only the sun's reflection on the calm water. He listened to the merlin until it was gone.

Like sound, the reflection would dissipate into dark waters in an hour or so. And someday there might not be any marsh here to catch reflections. You'll be long gone before that though. Okay, enough of these thoughts, this is no way to start the day, Samuel said aloud to the redbelly turtle shuffling out on the long end of a snag branch to wait for the sun. In a mile or so when he got to the levee trail, he saw a single hermit thrush singing from a pond apple tree growing up beside the canal. The Army Corp built the thirty-mile levee to keep the swamp from flooding into the western suburbs of Palm Beach County.

Four more of the thrushes sprang up from the pond apple tree. It was early September, and many of the passerine migrants had started to arrive. The merlin that Samuel heard earlier was one of the first wintering falcons to migrate south.

By this time of year, the Curlews might also have made their way south.

***

There was no end to the levee trail that runs straight south into the slash pines charred black by the Jarstorm wildfire two winters earlier. Atop the levee made by man to hold back wetlands, the trail ran as straight as a plum line. The photographer of birds kept hiking as the sun crept over everything. Unlike the forests of Solitudo County or the bluff pines of South Carolina, this wild land was flat, stretching for miles in every direction: to the east through the dry prairie and scrub forest and to the west through the lonely cypress swamp, and far to the south through the slash pines.

***

He crossed over the wooden trestle across the canal and its dry floodways. And he hiked further west onto another two track, this one with the grass growing nearly as tall as his waist off to both sides of the tracks. He was in the marsh swamp.

There was another thrush on a cattail. Unassuming and dull in her brown-gray plumage, she sang her lovely, melancholy song. Below the cattail, four or five feet away, a moccasin ripped across the water. The moccasin chose escape, swiveling so quickly across the top of the water that only ripples remained and a fear in Samuel's veins. It was a fear he had not known before he had seen the triangular head lunging at him from under the pine branch back in Solitudo County, a fear like an instinct that stayed there in his veins even after the water was smooth again.

***

Samuel could not look away from the water, and he was making his way back towards the two-track trail that led to the trestle bridge, when he saw the sky's reflection dim over the water, and he looked to the east. The sky turned darker, a storm coming in over the Atlantic. It was one of those late afternoons when the light just seemed to spill from the air, except for a low glow like a beam from a distant spotlight over the swamp waters to the west. He was three miles from the bridge and another five from camp. He picked up his pace trying to cover ground, but the rain started, beating down. The wind began to blow. His head down, he hiked that last half-mile to the trestle, the bridge hidden in the dense white fog of the rain.

For that last half-mile, it came down harder with each step, until finally he could see the bridge through the fog. Under the shelter, he shed his shirt soaked-through. It was twenty degrees colder than it was an hour earlier. He reached for the long-sleeve shirt rolled in his pack, but it was damp from the water that leaked in. He stood up and he felt the cold. Trying to keep warm, he paced, and put his hands out to do a few vertical pushups from the thick trestle brace. It didn't keep him much warmer.

He thought of waiting out the rain a long time ago as a boy, waiting against the bark of the old Oak as the rain slanted through a gray sky. He remembered the cold wind against his wet skin, the rain beating down above him. That was a long time ago, and he was different, and he was not different. It was not so long ago—when he really thought about it. No, it was not too long ago, but so much has happened since then. Sitting under the wood of the trestle bridge, Samuel thought about all the beautiful things he has seen, etched in his mind like the bark lines in that old Oak.

He woke just before midnight, under the trestles. The rain had stopped, but it was a cold, cloudy night with the moon a blur behind the cloud cover. He packed everything up and hiked the rest of the way back to camp. He settled into his tent, changing out of his damp clothes, and as he put the dry socks on, he felt just like he had come in from a day wandering back behind his parents' house a long time ago.

PUBLISHER'S NOTE

Now that you have finished reading this book, the author would be most grateful if you would take the time to post an honest review of it on Amazon, Barnes & Nobel or any other online bookseller's web site.

Anyone with an Amazon account can post reviews, even if you purchased the book somewhere else. If you ever purchased anything on Amazon, you have an account. A fair, objective and authentic review is requested so others may benefit from your opinion. It need not be long, just a couple of well chosen sentences can be enough to help potential readers decide if the book is worth their time. Your opinion is valuable to both the author and the publisher.

The author-publisher team put a lot of effort into editing the manuscript before publication, but no book is perfect. If you notice an error, you could help improve future editions by emailing us with the page number and line so it can be corrected.

Finally, if you enjoyed the book, be sure to tell your friends about it, in person and on social media such as Facebook, Twitter, LinkedIn and others.

Gene D. Robinson
publisher@moonshinecovepublishing.com

www.ingramcontent.com/pod-product-compliance
Lightning Source LLC
Chambersburg PA
BHW070819180626
6818CB00001B/332